IN THE NOW

KELLY SINCLAIR

LETHE PRESS
MAPLE SHADE, NEW JERSEY

Published by LETHE PRESS
118 Heritage Ave, Maple Shade, NJ 08052
lethepressbooks.com

ISBN 978-1-59021-462-6

Cover and interior design
by MATT CRESSWELL (INKSPIRAL DESIGN)

Kogarashi yo
nare ga yuku no
shizukesa no
omokage yumeni
iza kono nen

O winter wind
Tonight I shall sleep and dream
of the stillness
of that landscape where you reach
your final destination.

Ochiai Naobumi (d. 1903)

P R O L O G U E

ANOTHER TEDIOUS ARGUMENT, ONE HE AND HIS WIFE, MITSUI, HAD STARTED WITHOUT *even trying. The argument pretended to be about him being too old to take up a new career. Her real complaint went far deeper.*

Too much sukotchi-rokkusu in his belly, too many wild, smelly trucks in the Shinjuku, too many tourists crowding the streets. The Olympics meant nothing but an excuse for buying geisha dolls that were cheaper than in the Ginza district.

Watanabe Isao staggered out of the bar into the rain-dampened street. Mitsui might have been chattering behind him. He didn't care. He brushed back a hostess who seemed more concerned about smearing her garish mascara than losing a customer. There were hundreds of customers to take his place and that many more bars to visit. The burning in his throat intensified, fed by neon markers dazzling their cold fire at his every step.

"Why stop at being Koreya's radical waki? Go become a dancer, Isao!"

Mitsui's voice sounded very close.

"I wasn't his waki. I played the fool in a modern King Lear. I told you already," he said as he wheeled about.

A plump African woman, startled by their sudden closeness, backed into the arms of her pale boyfriend.

Gods, he needed something wet on his tongue. Becoming a dancer had been a youthful dream. Grenade shrapnel in his knee removed all such ambitions, leaving behind a husk possessing superb reflexes and balletic grace, neither of which helped him draw radios for Takeshita Electronic's advertising department. Why wouldn't he welcome the chance to escape all that, to become an actor?

Mitsui tepidly applauded his performance in Yoshiyuke's "Find Hakamadare," for which he received excellent reviews in Asahi Shimbun. As it turned out, the company's assistant director captured all Mitsui's attention. Why this scene? The entire company knew that she had a lover. How could he not have known? Except that he hadn't known until last night, when the dresser, whether in a spirit of pity or malice, whispered it to him before the second act.

Isao liked being drunk. The African woman's lover, with the well-fed look of an American, said something in that impossible, squirmy language, then stepped toward him. To fight? They had already won the war. What more did they want?

"Please don't trouble yourself, honorable gaijin. I will respectfully remove myself from your presence." He heaped on more sarcasm with an exaggerated bow.

Mitsui's eyes narrowed with disgust. He learned his role well from a hundred matinees watched over the years. Isao had now been cast as the outraged husband, the cuckold. He needed to recite his lines and watch, impotently, while she left him for another man. But first, he really needed another drink.

The male gaijin plucked at Isao's sleeve. That deserved a slap. Isao aimed his hand in the right direction, but instead, he slipped to the pavement.

"I killed your brothers and you still won't leave me alone." He managed to come to rest on his good knee. "All of you, go away, go away."

He must have screamed that, for a graybeard was trying to pull him back onto the sidewalk.

A sound pierced through the din. A truck horn, very near. He took one step away from the graybeard, and something lifted him into the sky. Lights—cheery lights—a rush of wind through his hair, then oblivion.

O N E

IT HAD BEEN A GOOD, VERGING ON EXCELLENT, DAY, AMY DURAN THOUGHT AS SHE pulled her Honda into the driveway.

She resolved the author-scheduling clash that slotted the feminist blogging workshop right before a Zen hunting seminar, thereby averting a bloodbath in Bookish's meeting room. Not only that, she listened as her boss overshared as usual about his latest dating melodrama without her once offering a fix-it. That was something Carla—Dr. Turner—stressed during their last session.

"Solving other people's problems is no substitute for addressing your own issues," the psychiatrist said.

Amy kept her mouth shut, hadn't she, except at lunchtime, when she finished half a tofu wrap without feeling as though she needed a ten-mile run to sweat it out of her system. As she walked up to her front door, she noticed a hopeful green sprout next to the sidewalk and wondered how she had overlooked it. Austin weather kept weeds growing almost year round.

She changed into her gardening shorts, careful to keep her eyes averted from the antique full-length mirror in the far corner of her bedroom. The mirror had been so handy back when she daily monitored the state of her hips, but now it served as a reminder of the mess she'd made of her life.

Things were different now, weren't they? Yet, she still dreaded seeing herself exposed in flesh and bone. *Y otra cosa*, why did she even have the thing in her bedroom if she was so afraid of it?

She skip-moved the mirror down the hall and into the middle bedroom, used mainly for guests and folding clothes, and set it down in a corner.

She caught a glimpse of herself before she turned away. She still had cheekbones, thank goodness—twin Guatemalan peaks that came courtesy of her late father—but the hips. Awful. No, not awful. Believe in Dr. Turner, not that nagging voice. She was doing better, so *cayete*.

I LOOKED FORWARD TO MIKE ZILINSKY'S E-MAILS. A TYPICAL ONE LED OFF WITH "CARLA, YOU WON'T BELIEVE THIS." There'd be a satirical article from the *Onion* website about Texas's governor coming out as being gay, and a gay alien, at that. That was Mike for you. In his running daydream of our '70s cop show, he cast me as Carla "Chocolicious" Turner, the wise, responsible partner to his nutjob detective. Even back in the Army, where we served as psychiatrists to war-shattered soldiers, Mike brought light and energy to our grinding schedule.

We discovered how simpatico we were as running buddies and Nintendo warriors. I don't recall him, before we both found wives, practicing his lover boy pitch on me. Even then, he knew that to be a pointless exercise. We segued seamlessly into civilian life. He went on to coordinate research trials for Borlauch, the pharmaceutical giant, and I settled into private practice in Austin.

Every few months, he'd fly in from Chicago on a work-related excuse. After going out for tacos at Guero's or some other *masa* heaven, we'd finish the evening with drafts and darts at a local pub. Although it began as a foursome, he went through an acrimonious divorce from his wife, while I had to learn to live without my wife, Isabelle, who died much too young of breast cancer.

Drafts and darts, occasional ballgames at the Drum, phone-calls, e-mails, and textings framed our friendship. My older brother long ago banished me from his life over many issues, my sexuality being but one of them. Since Belle was an only child, Mike's self-promotion to uncle worked out for everyone.

The girls eagerly looked forward to his visits. Rashida refused to acknowledge her crush on him until she graduated from high school. As a self-assured UT freshman, she laughed it off as a normal phase. It had something with his curly black hair, me speaking as an objective witness, and his athletic physique. He took it in good humor and never cracked any jokes at Rashida's expense.

Imani, on the cusp of fifteen, and a mass of lanky elbows and braids, worshipped him with no apparent overtones of puppy love.

Today's e-mail, however, hewed to a work-related topic rather than faux aliens. I sometimes worked with Mike on local test studies for Borlauch drug research, so I was interested when he e-mailed me about a new treatment for substance abuse. The attachments he included in the e-mail made beta-anodynol sound like a miracle drug.

Used in conjunction with hypnosis, beta-anodynol achieved sedation with no apparent impact on heart rate and blood pressure. Mike went into it further over the phone.

"With beta-anodynol, you create a hypersuggestible state in your client, making induction much easier to initiate. Frankly, Carla, whatever you tell them, they believe, absolutely. It hits quick, leaves quick, and it doesn't blitz them like other drugs we've tried. We're talking maximum efficacy and one hundred percent compliance. Every participant in our studies over the past five years has stayed with it—and these are abusers bounced from every treatment program out there."

"If it's so great, why is this the first I've heard about it?"

"The original project head quit to work for the government. They're looking at their own applications for it. My boss, Dr. Nyanga, shifted me over, which took her long enough. I've been hearing rumors about it for years."

"What about side effects?"

"Biggest one is mild nausea, but only six percent experience it. Next ones after that are photosensitivity and vertigo. Which amounts to a rounding error, when you consider how some clients would report a side effect to drinking water."

Since Borlauch had pulled strings to expedite bringing the drug to market, full FDA approval for use in treatment of substance abusers was slated later in the fall. The company now had designs on the larger, more lucrative market of smokers, people with eating disorders, and obsessive-compulsives.

"The reporting of side effects is certain to go up," I said. "OCDs tend to be hypochondriacs, and heavy smokers already have compromised immune systems."

"Oh yeah, I'm expecting an uptick in symptoms."

Mike planned to start with a small test study to work out any glitches in protocol, followed by a major FDA-convincing study.

I thought hypnotherapy had been oversold to the public. "For $50, Dr. So and So will change your life!" For the handful of my clients requesting that approach, I found it to be. at best, modestly helpful.

It made me think of Amy Duran, a bookseller by trade. I'd been treating her for years, working with her in managing her anorexia.

While various therapeutic modalities can treat anorexia, it is a stubborn, deeply rooted behavior. Behavioral disorders are never "cured." The best one hopes for is to reduce the relapses and manage stressors.

Beta-anodynol sounded too much like a snake-oil nostrum, but even if the benefits lasted no longer than five years, that represented five years of progress in therapy. When Mike proposed bringing me some samples, I didn't hesitate to accept.

That evening, with an OWN network talk show as background noise, Rashida, Imani, and I made smothered chicken and rice, layered salad, and, Imani's favorite, sweet potato pie. Although we tried not to get in each other's way, we didn't always succeed. Three busy schedules rarely allow for group cooking or sit-down meals period. But with Imani fresh out of school for the summer, we were enjoying the time together, give or take a blow-up over who rinsed the grater last.

Imani chattered nonstop about her upcoming stay in Memphis with Belle's parents where she would be playing AAU basketball. The last six weeks of school had been something of a trial for the both of us, but she emerged with all A's, except for a B in history. How could she tell me Sheryl Swoopes's life story, yet fail to remember who fought the War of 1812?

"Mama?" Imani turned up the sound on the television. "Do you believe in reincarnation?"

"Of course not, baby."

A smooth voice more velveteen than velvet escaped from the monitor speakers. I recognized it immediately—Dr. Faye Marin, my old UT psych professor. Every couple of years, she produced a bestseller vapor-thin on the problems and vapid in their solutions.

Abusive husbands. Near-death survivors. Battling one's personal demons. If it was trendy, Marin could be relied upon to profit from ambient cultural fears. From what I heard from fellow alumni, she'd raked in enough money to afford a home in the River Oaks area in Houston. Still brunette and unlined, however botoxed, Marin looked as sleek and regal as she did decades ago.

The show's host had her on the ropes over a recent bogus claim of past-life regression by a Swedish writer.

Marin tried for a positive spin. "I wouldn't judge the entire field by the actions of one charlatan. Regression therapy is but one pathway in my collaboration with the patient, or, as I prefer to say, 'explorer.'"

I felt the way a Catholic might upon hearing a priest's renunciation of vows—upset, even though I'd long tagged her as a media personality better suited for the camera than the classroom. Her snobbishness and devotion to favored students too often had rubbed me raw.

She blatted on and on about future lives, past lives, and the impact karma has on one's next reincarnation.

"You're speaking to a Western audience, Dr. Marin." The host steered her guest back to port. "Would you explain what you mean by choosing your karma?"

"Oh, yes," Marin said brightly. "There's a decisive act or series of acts which happen before you die—sometimes right before the passage, sometimes many years before—they fix where you go in your next life. Hindus and Buddhists are quite familiar with this."

"What you're saying is that if you're cruel to animals, you'll come back as a stray cat."

"That's a simplified reading, but yes, there's a consequence to your actions—"

"Hell," I said.

That provoked a dig in my side from Rashida.

"In my sessions we investigate the critical choices a person made in his or her past life. If you've tried to lead an enlightened existence, for instance, given to the poor, if you've tried to maintain the balance between right actions and wrong actions, your next life reflects this overall growth."

"You become a millionaire, is that what you're saying?" The host said with a disbelieving smile. There were hoots from the audience.

Rashida dug into my ribs again. "Oprah must've lived a lot of good lives before this one."

According to Marin, Belle, a lifelong Methodist and chronic do-gooder, should be punished for the sins of her past life. Belle, who cried over fallen baby sparrows. My wife, who was so much more than my better half. My heart, my soul. And to think Marin made a living off marginalizing the suffering of others.

I confiscated the remote control and switched to a documentary on black filmmakers.

"Mama?" Imani gave the stirring spoon a long, contemplative lick. "Can people really be hypnotized like that? Where they can go back to Egypt and see Cleopatra? It'd be so neat to see stuff that happened a thousand years ago."

"Over two thousand years ago," Rashida, my teacher-in-training, corrected.

"'Mani, hypnosis doesn't work that way," I told her. "It's not so much a trance, as people tend to believe. They're not asleep when they're hypnotized. It's more like daydreaming."

"So those patients—"

"Clients."

"Clients... they're dreaming they're in Egypt, but they're making it up." Imani's face clouded.

"They may not know that they're confabulating or inventing their memories, but when you have someone like Dr. Marin guiding them, they're in trouble. She wants them to have a past life, fake or not."

"And you best believe they'll have one," Rashida said. "You want me to leave off the onions on the chicken?"

"No, let's live dangerously."

The idea grew, as I drove down Lamar Boulevard the next morning through a drowsy rain. I turned on to Fourth Street, then onto a quiet block of cafes and cut-glassed offices. I shared a suite and office manager with three other professionals.

My plan: I would debunk Marin's reincarnation hoax by using Mike's new drug. Give the beta-anodynol to a non-believer in reincarnation. Mike, for instance. Regress him to fuzzy early childhood consciousness. Seek to go farther back, without implanting suggestions, without encouraging the invention of so-called other lives, and watch as the door fails to open. Without lies, without wishful thinking, reincarnation would be revealed to be a sham and its advocates con artists, or at best, dupes.

I'd then write up a summation and send an e-mail to Marin's Web site. Unlikely she'd respond, but she'd know one of her former students was on to her game.

I greeted the office manager and collected a cup of green tea from her en route to my desk. I booted up my computer and checked messages.

Mike e-mailed that he'd be in town on Wednesday, so would I have a client on hand at that time?

I thought of one of my obese patients, who'd been making fitful progress since first coming to my office last year. But, again, the image of Amy Duran returned to my mind.

A fine-boned woman in her early forties, Amy first entered my office when her battle with anorexia had reached a crisis point. She somehow forced herself to make an appointment, and, even more miraculously, appeared at my office without her family and friends having shanghaied her into it.

Amy possessed an underlying strength, a stability rarely shared by other anorexics who pass through my door. Together we sought out the stress points in her life, including her position teaching English literature to high school students and the staleness of her relationship with a real-estate baroness.

She slowly began to share painful childhood memories of her father, who hung himself in the attic while she and her brother watched television in the den, and her mother, who thereafter refused to mention his name.

Amy accepted that her love of books had not translated into enjoyment of a packed teaching schedule and that she would benefit from a change in careers. Business classes helped her transition into working at Bookish, a large, yet eclectic, multistory bookstore with an equally diverse clientele.

It was on that parking lot of Bookish where Amy broke with her lover. The after-effects of that clash played out for months, but she came out of it better able to cope with her problems.

Too often, those who struggle with eating disorders refuse to allow intervention, thus avoiding any diminution of their self-control. Amy beat the odds to the point that she had become a twice-monthly date on my calendar. She visited more often as warranted, but it had been over two years since the last relapse.

When I called her at home, Amy at first sounded dubious about participating in a research study. I conscientiously ran through the list of possible side effects.

"It sounds safe enough. You said it's free?" She spoke in her usual murmur.

"Everything is, including the treatment, the session, and the follow-up in six months. Paid for by the drug company."

"Um, why me?"

"You've made steady progress over the years. This treatment could possibly provide a little help. Since you're already scheduled for Wednesday afternoon, what I'm asking is for you to leave work a little earlier and stay at the office an hour longer than usual. There'll be some paperwork to fill out before the session."

"It might be fun. What have I got to lose?" I could almost hear her shrug.

T W ☉

MIKE BROUGHT A TATTERED PACKAGE WITH HIM FROM CHICAGO. AIRPORT security made him unwrap it at both ends of the trip. He commissioned a painter—artist was too strong a word for the level of ability involved—to paint a portrait of the girls and me. The painter had copied a studio photograph sent to him last year.

Looking at the Carla in the painting, I had to smile at the painter's generosity in giving me dimples, although why he or she made me shades lighter than my usual coffee-no-cream complexion, best not to speculate. I thanked my friend and resolved to place the painting in the study, deciding not to inflict it upon visitors.

While driving us over to Guero's taco place, I laid out my idea for refuting Faye Marin.

He took a few seconds to respond, which for Mike was a good sign. His bullshit barometer usually kicked in on the spot.

"Nyanga absolutely hates that stuff," he said.

Dr. Nyanga was Mike's boss at Borlauch.

"So she wouldn't want to do it."

"What I mean is she can't stand pseudo-science. Says it reminds her of how some people back home in Kenya still believe in demons. It really bugs her that here, where we live in a high-tech society, people read horoscopes and call psychic lines, even more obsessed with ghosts than so-called backward cultures. She'll agree; count on it. In fact, I know she'd love us to record it for the next project get-together. I'll call her tonight and run it by her."

Although I didn't much like the idea of being part of the show, Mike thought it the perfect kiss-off note for a media junkie like Marin.

"There's no way Marin would show it to anyone, Carla. You think she'd want people to know she's a phony? No way. It might even shut her up for a while."

The next morning, after waffles with Mike and the girls, I headed to work while he met with several other psychiatrists with whom Borlauch had a study agreement. When he showed up at four, everything was ready for the previously arranged induction.

I prepared my part of the set-up, which consisted of a set of earbuds connected up to a sound system and my headset.

Mike laid out his injectable supplies. "Where's the gold watch?"

"We could use your Rolex. Nah, I have them listen to a nature sounds CD, then my voice comes in. Keeps them focused. Music's boring as hell, but seems to work okay."

Mike brandished the syringe.

"This will make it a breeze. What we found is that since you don't have to spend any time relaxing them, the talk-down is minimal. But, if you want to give them the old 'relax your feet, relax your legs' routine, go right ahead. They probably expect it."

It should have concerned me that a drug could be so effective, but this was Mike Zilinsky talking to me, not a government researcher bent on mind-control.

Amy came in at that moment, surprised by the sight of a stranger wielding a needle. She was dressed in white slacks, a pale blue blouse, and black silk vest.

"Come on in."

Amy gave Mike a sideways glance then found her seat and began filling out the forms. Even for an apparently safe drug, it makes sense to have the subject fill out the usual waivers, although my clients' experience with Borlauch drug studies have largely been free of adverse reactions

A thin, alert woman, Amy possessed almond-shaped eyes that she once said came courtesy of her late father, a Guatemalan immigrant who reluctantly allowed his children to learn Spanish despite his Anglo wife's enthusiasm for bilingualism.

The woman who came into my office smiled timidly at me, and her chocolate brown hair possessed a glossy sheen that had been absent during her crisis phase.

During that phase, she displayed signs of a deepening romantic attachment to me. Those signals eventually subsided. She never knew how close her feelings came to being returned, so utterly lost I felt after the death of my wife.

I remembered Belle back in the good years. I liked that nuclear unit feeling, the warmth of being there, totally there, for our girls, so unlike my absent father and two-jobs-never-home mother.

"The child is parent to the adult," my Psych One professor—Faye Marin—proclaimed in her usual know-it-all fashion. Utter nonsense. This child earned a bachelor's degree, let the Army pay the rest of the way, and moved on after the payback time. I succeeded with little to no help from my parents, and, needless to say, without any professional assist from Marin.

Tuning back into the conversation, I realized too late Mike had asked Amy her opinion on reincarnation. I frowned my disapproval at him. He'd already agreed to be the test subject.

She blinked thoughtfully and answered in her usual tentative manner.

"Really, um, I don't believe in it? Not before I converted to Judaism and certainly not after. It sounds like an easy way out, but it's not logical."

I took Mike outside the office for a talkdown. Not the first time in our long friendship that his enthusiasm outflew his common sense.

"You said you'd do it," I said.

"I'm thinking, we have someone who's signed the waivers, someone who's not in the profession. You know Marin will blow us off if I'm the subject. She'll call it a hatchet job. Besides, Ms. Duran will look great on camera."

I got him to agree to postpone discussion of our debunking until later.

First, session number one. As the music played in her headphones, I injected the beta-anodynol, gave it the suggested twenty minutes to work, and began. Gradually, she seemed to fade from herself, and I had to repeat my initial words to get her attention. But after that, she listened with a childlike gravity.

The simple phrases I spoke—to know that she was not fat, to accept that she could not control every aspect of her body and her life, and to be at peace with her physical self-image—mantras spoken softly into a microphone and into her ears. They registered on her face as empirical fact. But would it still work in six weeks, a year, or a lifetime?

AMY KNEW WITH ABSOLUTE CLARITY THAT DR. TURNER WAS THE PERFECT doctor. No, she was far more than that. Beautiful, brilliant, anything out of her mouth had to be true.

Each word resonated through the room, rumbling, picking up strength until it washed over Amy in an aural flood of baptismal waters. Amy had never felt more alive than at that moment, yet at the same time so relaxed, so free of worry.

Of course, she was a normal woman with normal appetites. If she gained a pound, it didn't mean the end of the world. The more Amy listened, the more plausible it seemed that she had only to breathe in, breathe out, live her life, release the negative emotions, accept who she was, breathe in, breathe out.

IT SEEMED OVER IN A MOMENT, BUT THE SESSION, INCLUDING THE WARM-UP and warm-down, lasted over an hour. When I suggested to Amy that she return to wakefulness, her eyes popped open.

Mike latched on to her immediately.

"How do you feel? Do you sense any difference in your self-image?"

I shushed him., thinking that lingering traces of beta-anodynol in her bloodstream might cause her to invent differences in order to please Mike.

She mumbled that she needed something to eat. I scammed a couple of oatmeal cookies from a mini-fridge behind the office manager's desk and delivered them to Amy.

Matter-of-factly, she consumed the cookies.

"I feel comfortable, as though it's nothing out of the ordinary." She wiped the crumbs from her hands. "I hate to eat and run, but I need to get going."

"Are you sure about coming tomorrow?" Mike asked. "We'll be recording it. It's not for public use, but your face will be seen."

"You don't need to do it," I interjected. "It's more of a lark than an experiment. I'm sure you're too busy—"

"Dr. Turner." Formal as always. "It's all right. Dr. Zilinsky? I'm pleased to help you disprove reincarnation. It's the least I can do."

EVERY BLOCK, AMY DROVE BY ANOTHER FAST-FOOD PLACE AND ANOTHER restaurant. Every block, she tested herself with images of fried chicken, enchiladas, donuts, snow cones, a sign for *phở,* a Vietnamese dish—what she wanted, what scared her, what made her try to block out the view—but all the way back to work, the utter normality of the drive bore into her.

It's just food; that's all. Eat it; don't eat it. One big nothing, as her nephew, Randall, liked to say. As she turned into the parking lot of Bookish, she saw an obese man standing outside the entrance.

Something's coming, she wanted to tell him, something's coming that will save you. If not for the fact it would have been totally out of character, she wanted to roll down the window and shout out the good news. Quickly, she uttered a *shehecheyanu,* always good to recite on joyous occasions. Everything came from God, so this came from God, even if it did take a circuitous route.

"Thank you, Dr. Turner," she whispered.

IN THE NOW

THE REST OF THE AFTERNOON FLEW BY. AFTER MIKE WENT OFF TO LOOK FOR A tripod to use with my camcorder, I keyed in some notes about the session, killing time until my next client, an overweight woman I'd originally considered for Mike's session.

She'd been doing fairly well on her behavior modification routines and antidepressants, but recently experienced a relapse. She knew her problem areas and seemed to be making a sincere effort but, during the session, I wondered if Mike was correct that a shot of beta-anodynol and a few choice words could cure her.

One session, one shot, one cure. That couldn't possibly be the case. Perhaps addicts, desperate to avoid incarceration, had extra motivation to stay clean after beta-anodynol treatment. Wait until completion of a full-scale study. After that, we would know how well the drug worked. Amy, however, believed that she'd been healed.

When I got home, Rashida was upstairs helping Imani pack. My oldest, in from her part-time job at the hemp store, told us how a gaggle of teens came in to sniff the purses before she ran them off.

"Mama, you should have seen them. Boys with skeezer haircuts, carrying skateboards. I set them straight or tried to. They looked so disappointed when they left. One of the boys came back in and bought a tube of lip-gloss. He said his lips got chapped when he was out riding. I'm still not convinced he didn't try to eat it."

Restless for tomorrow's trip, Imani sighed during Rashida's account. Her mood didn't improve upon hearing that Uncle Mike opted for dinner with Dr. Toni Akugawa, a psychiatrist he was wooing. Whether for Borlauch or himself, I wasn't altogether certain.

I sat on the bed as Imani rolled socks, ever so precise in getting the fold just right. She looked at that moment unnervingly like Belle the first time we met, when she was a newly divorced mother and a sought-after college professor. Belle had been the genius in our family, but she was also the one who died first, and soon the girls would be grown and out of the house.

Gently pulling Imani over to me, I gave her a hug.

"I won't be gone that long." She snuggled closer.

We ate a quick supper of smothered chicken recycled into wraps, then Rashida left for what she called a study session with her friends at their favorite coffeehouse. Not only did she design her own reading course for the summer, she also dragooned her buddies into following along. Tonight, they were dissecting

Heart of Darkness. Poor Joe Conrad.

I dropped Imani off at her best friend's house, where they'd planned a video game marathon as a sendoff for the basketball warrior. As she got out of the car, Imani ducked her head back in for a moment.

"You better not change things around while I'm gone. Don't be renting out my room."

"We could make some money doing that."

"Uh-uh."

THREE

WHILE WORKING ALPHABETIZED STACKS OF THE DAY'S INVOICES AND PUBLICITY packets, Amy thought of how her brother, Gordon, would react to yesterday's events. His staid little sister, whose only departure from the norm thus far had been converting to Judaism, participated in a drug research study.

Gordon, who kept his jet-black hair in a ponytail, possessed a more adventurous streak. He recently made a midlife career move from money management to working as an art collector/middle man and photographer.

By following his financial advice, she'd cashed out most of her portfolio at what turned out to be the perfect time. This allowed her career change to the less-stressful book trade. A soft landing made possible by her brother and Dr. Turner.

The move freed her from the daily torture of teaching literature to indifferent sixteen-year-olds. Some made an effort, however limp, to grasp Edgar Allan Poe. Amy was the one who didn't belong.

As her best friend, Nina, pointed out, "You're wrapped too tight."

To which she could reply that Nina hadn't the first clue about managing her music career or finances, for that matter, so they both had control issues—too much and too little. Thank God for Dr. Turner. Amy couldn't conceive of what her life would have been like if she hadn't entered therapy.

She remembered those awkward first weeks of wanting to make a good impression, not to appear as crazy as she felt, but next came the gradual letting go. She stopped caring that she was crying in front of another human being, revealing the utter pettiness of her life and complaints.

What did Dr. Turner say during those weeks? Amy couldn't remember anything except thinking that she was runway model beautiful. Odd how hypnosis reproduced that early impression.

A savior mentality, she guessed, idolizing the one who saves you from drowning, the saint who over time shrank to normal dimensions. At some point, Amy noticed a framed photograph of her family and asked about the partner, only to learn that she had died within the past year. How fortunate that Dr. Turner never noticed her idol-making phase.

Amy didn't see any point to the night's past-life experiment. A test case would change the mind of no true believer, yet she'd do anything for her miracle workers. Anything.

A blanketing quiet had settled into her mind, muting any traces of body anxiety. She sought out traces of the putdown artist. There were faint residues of a sneer, phrases of contempt remembered at a great remove, as though she'd witnessed it many years ago. She felt... totally unlike herself.

She couldn't wait to tell Gordon and her nephew, Randall, her friend Nina, Rabbi Fleischer, and anyone else who might care, except that it'd be best to wait until after the night's session. That way she could present it as one uninterrupted story.

No messy digressions, no quaint tales like the ones Mama used to unreel. Even on her deathbed, Mama couldn't come to the point about what she wanted for the funeral. Gordon guided her through the details, yet still he and Amy had to hear one more time how their grandmother burned all the linen and furniture in the room where an aunt succumbed to tuberculosis, then came a tale about Mama's San Antonio neighborhood party after the defeat of a hated politician.

Amy would have preferred a personal conversation with her mother, some kind of closure, but the last coherent words from Mama's lips were, "Mom told him nobody in the family would ever vote for him again."

Not exactly words of wisdom.

MIKE HAD TAKEN ADVANTAGE OF HIS COPY OF MY OFFICE KEY TO SET UP THE camcorder on a tripod. He assured me that he would use normal room lighting to reduce the tension for Amy.

"Pretend the camera's not there." Mike had noticed my level of distraction.

"Right. Knowing that little red light will be on, not a problem."

Mike eliminated the light with a piece of duct tape.

This experiment by no means was a fait accompli simply because nonbelievers were involved. Since we all bathe in our culture's stream of supernatural memes,

I couldn't mention possible spirit guides or other loaded subjects. Under the influence of the drug and my words, an otherwise rational Amy might well invent an army of angels.

About the previous day's session, Mike had heard back from the director, Dr. Nyanga, who gave the go-ahead to his setting up a full trial in Austin. I would join several other doctors in providing the test subjects and aftercare.

Based on the reports I read, Borlauch had sufficiently tweaked dosage levels in earlier studies so that possible adverse drug interactions were largely confined to clients taking MAO inhibitors, which I rarely prescribe. Newer drugs are as effective in treating major depression without MAOI's adverse interactions.

"I've read the studies, Mike. Borlauch has given multiple doses to subjects, but what about twice in twenty-four hours?"

"You have nothing to worry about. Beta-anodynol works as advertised. Infield singles, no home runs."

"Not really a baseball fan."

"And yet we still hang out together. Amazing. The drug works fast, leaves fast. We did a study in Cleveland where test subjects received seven doses in seven days. Results were the same each time. No hangover, no drowsiness."

He saw my worried expression. "Once you eliminate the eating behavior, you can devote more time to exploring the underlying trauma and to weaning them off various medications."

He kept fiddling with the tripod. "I doubt that beta-anodynol will ever be indicated for the truly messy stuff."

"Bulimia and anorexia aren't messy enough?" I asked.

"When you get down to it, they're not that complicated. All beta-anodynol does is remove a negative sound byte from their head."

"And insert a new one."

"A healthy sound byte, one that repeats what their doctor has been saying for years."

Amy arrived just after seven, about to finish off a gyro.

"Sorry, I had to stay longer than I'd anticipated. I was quite hungry."

She folded the wrapper methodically then arched it into the trash basket.

"It looks as though the positive effects of the treatment are continuing." Unstoppable Mike.

She nodded in lieu of speaking, which was a typical response for her. She sat down in the armchair, and put on the headphones.

While I welcomed the chance to debunk Marin, did our subject have to be Amy? She tapped the side of the chair in a steady metronome, ready for us to begin.

"You don't have to do this," I told her.

"For the first time since forever, I ate breakfast without worrying about the calories. It didn't even cross my mind. To me, what you're doing tonight is pretty much what you did yesterday. People like that doctor you mentioned, she pushes diets and the latest fads, like past lives. She takes advantage of people when they're weak. You're telling her, enough already, so I'm glad to help out."

After Mike administered the injection, I turned off the overhead light and adjusted the corner lamp to an off-focus. I pulled my chair to where I could remote-control the CD volume and still have a full view of the subject.

I allowed a few minutes for the drug to circulate in her system. After that, nothing else could delay the procedure, so I cleared my mind of extraneous thoughts, recalled my notes, and proceeded.

Feel your legs starting to relax... feel the stress of the day slip away... standard relaxation phrases that appeared to work instantly and another textbook example of Mike's so-called chemical inductions.

It crossed my mind that I could skip the intermediate stages and ask her if she remembered anything before her birth. Why bother with any build-up? But, with the camcorder, Dr. Nyanga's amanuensis, at work, we needed to observe tradition.

Back we went down the ladder of years, to her life as a teacher, sliding back to her days at the University of Texas, pausing for a pre-teen Amy taking violin lessons from an elderly Hungarian woman.

"Paprika." She wrinkled her nose. "The whole house smells like paprika and Brahms."

"Brahms smells like paprika?" I couldn't help but ask.

"Oh yeah," Amy said in an indolent manner. "Brahms is okay, I guess, but Schubert is cool."

We took the next step back with care. Not the year she turned seven, for that was the minefield of her father's suicide. I would have her visit ages six, four, then three.

"PAPA?"

Papa was in a bad, bad mood, mad about something. He kept staring at Mama, who was washing dishes. He promised to take Amy and Gordy for a chocolate shake at Hut's. He promised, but then he said she made too much noise cleaning off the table, so no trip in the car.

Could she go outside? She couldn't tell from the way he looked. Sometimes he yelled about the littlest thing, and sometimes he didn't care if she knocked over a plant.

"Papa? I'll be good, I'll be good forever if you let me go out and play. I'm sorry I made noise."

Turning to say something, he faded into nothingness, replaced by her brother.

"*Mire, mire.*" Gordy lifted up a mud pie. Water from the drainage ditch dripped from his hands.

"*Es muy grande*, my pie is the best, *si*? You have that hole in the middle. Like a donut, *verdad*? Maybe you should make donuts, not pies."

The sun is *muy, muy caliente.*

"Mama," she cried out. "I wanna drink of *limonada.*"

INTERESTING HOW AMY EXPERIENCED THE EVENTS NOT AS A CLOSE OBSERVER, but as a direct participant. I wondered how well this drug-accentuated behavior would work with her pre-verbal memories. The adult Amy had to emerge in order to act as mediator.

"Go back farther, go as far back as you can, and tell me what you see."

Pop-eyed and dazed, she bore the look of a toddler first unleashed on the world. Her face washed itself of expression, her hands and feet curled inward.

"Carla, she's in the womb." Mike's voice throbbed with excitement.

I covered the microphone and quieted him. "Don't be ridiculous. You don't know where she is right now. Let's take things slowly."

IMAGES SHIFTED IN AND OUT OF FOCUS BEFORE DISAPPEARING IN A BLUR. FLASHING sparklers pulsed to a buzzing drone that grew louder the further down she sank.

In a notime, in a nowhere, walls formed out of the motes of light into a tunnel. The drone became the rushing of a great stream that waved through her and around her, yet still like glowing embers in a shaft of afternoon sun.

She felt the presence of someone nearby, others farther away.

"Who are you?" she tried to ask the neighbor. She had a brief, confusing look at his face—so familiar, so strange—but an immense exhaustion quieted her thoughts.

All sensation veiled behind the mantilla of dreamtime.

SINCE AMY RESPONDED TO MY SUGGESTION BY ADOPTING AN INFANTILE STATE, I would have to rouse her and abandon the effort. The drug worked too well to be practical for our intentions. Amy wanted to please us. Asked to recall being a toddler, she became thoroughly child-like, which precluded adult Amy's participation. No past-life exposé, no slam dunk on Marin. Oh well. No harm, no foul. We had something to joke about afterward. Carla's harebrained idea.

"Amy, this is Dr. Turner."

Oddly rigid in her posture, she sat forward in her chair and opened her eyes.

"Amy—"

A low-pitched guttural sound burst forth from her lips, choppy and frantic, and completely unintelligible.

She tore off her headphones, stumbled to her feet, and stared at us and her surroundings with naked desperation. Another rapid stream of language came out of her as her whole body began to tremble.

"Carla." Mike stood by my side.

Without noticing it, I had risen to my feet.

I adopted a stronger tone. "Amy, this is Dr. Turner. I want you to wake up feeling well rested."

With a low cry, she rushed to the door and was out of the office before Mike and I could react. We followed her out onto the sidewalk and saw her sprint down the street. She reached the far side and disappeared behind a passing truck before we thought to give chase.

Minutes later, having lost track of her in an alley, we agreed to split up: Mike would continue to track her on foot while I went back for my car.

It being a clear, moonlit evening, there were numerous people out on the streets. They were more intent on partying than on troublemaking, but not everyone would benignly ignore a confused woman.

Knowing that Amy ran a couple of miles every day, and that she was in a manic or fugue state, I made a generous estimate of how far she could have gone. I also phoned Rashida at the coffeehouse. She asked what Amy was wearing and promised to find her.

"Don't worry, Mama. There'll be a lot of characters out tonight, but if she's as whack as you said, she'll still stand out."

After touring the Warehouse District, I turned closer to Sixth Street, all the while keeping in phone contact with a breathless, panicky Mike. Not that I felt any more relaxed by comparison.

"Does she have a history of doing this?" he asked.

"Of course not."

"I mean, is she bipolar, borderline, does she have a history of hysterical episodes, delusions, anything at all?"

"She's a reasonably well-adjusted, compensating anorexic, Mike. I'm sorry I can't come up with anything jazzier. The one major trauma in her life occurred in childhood when her father hung himself."

"She may be experiencing a post-traumatic stress episode."

"Maybe."

"No one's ever gone off like that. I swear to you, Carla. You read the reports."

I viewed that statement with certain fatalism. I knew since I ran the session and the session went bad, it would all come back on me, regardless of the sequence of events.

In the meantime, Amy was wandering around downtown Austin. I glanced at my watch. Nine o'clock. It wasn't the witching hour yet, but we needed to find her, and soon.

I thought back to the moment she'd opened her eyes. A stranger looked at me in a dead panic, certain that I meant trouble. I cursed aloud. The police.

A bored dispatcher took down the description: a thin woman suffering from a drug reaction. Confused, but not dangerous.

ISAO RAN ANOTHER BLOCK, THEN ANOTHER, HIS PACE QUICKENING AS HIS SURROUNDINGS blurred together into an incoherent mess.

No logic to his senses, just blood pulsing and strong, amazingly strong legs carrying him around groups of foreigners who reminded him of those strangers who tried to attack him in the room.

A well-built man with a beatnik haircut stepped in front of Isao and spoke in slow, measured tones, words that seemed to hang in the air, words without meaning.

Side-stepping the obstacle, Isao bounced off the glass wall of a brightly lit café where the diners sat gaping at him. Choosing a direction at random, he sped off again.

Even his wife, with her usual cruelties, would be a welcome sight.

A LITTLE OVER AN HOUR LATER, RASHIDA AND HER FRIENDS FOUND AMY HUDDLED in a doorway on Sixth Street, a few yards up from the Esther's Follies comedy venue. I called the police to wave them off before parking on a side street.

I nudged my way through the crowd, encountering Mike at Esther's giant window. An Elvis angel in a rush to go back inside almost ran both of us down.

"How does she look?" I asked Mike.

"Exhausted. There's that kid from the tattoo shop." He motioned at a young Asian man, adorned with piercings of his ears, nose, and eyebrows and sporting triabl tattoos on his forearms. "He said she came in trying to talk to him."

The young man patted my shoulder companionably.

"I'm sorry y'all lost your patient, but she looks okay to me. Kind of whupped, you know. Like, this isn't a night to go for a run. You could fall out from the humidity. I gave her a bottle of water."

"I appreciate that."

"You know, she doesn't look Korean."

"What?"

"She was trying to talk Korean to me, or Chinese, something like that. Yeah, like I'm supposed to know everything Asian. I can barely order off a menu in Vietnamese and this chick's trying to carry on a muy intense conversation. Freaked me out."

I noticed Rashida and her crew clustered in front of a darkened doorway. They were taking their roles as bodyguards seriously, their scowls firmly in place.

"I think he's on to something."

Mike's bellow in my ear cut through the bass-heavy riffs of a trip-blues band wailing a couple of doors down.

"She was talking in an Asiatic language. I didn't realize it at the time because she was speaking in such a rush."

"Mike, I realize you've seen more than your share of foreign movies, but I know for a fact that Amy's only other language was Spanish. She wished her father had taught her the Indian dialect he grew up speaking and told her something about that culture."

"She might have picked it up in early childhood and the session brought it out of her subconscious. In any case, she may have never told you she'd been studying another language."

Amy sat on her knees in a corner of the doorway, legs bent under her. She looked spent of strength and yet as wary as a wolf brought almost to bay. Her face and blouse were drenched with perspiration. She seemed not to care what we did, only that we came no closer.

In a rush, one of Rashida's friends arrived with a round Asian man in tow.

"We're in luck," she announced cheerfully. "This is Mickey from my film theory class. He speaks Chinese."

"Cantonese." His accent was pure Californian. "I'm not that good."

I scooted him closer to the doorway. We needed to eliminate one language and shoot holes in Mike's theory in order to follow up on the Indian dialect.

"What I need for you to do is say that it is time for her to wake up."

"Pardon me?"

"She was in a hypnotic state when this happened. I told her earlier in the session that when we were through I would tell her to wake up."

Even as I told him, I knew how ridiculous it sounded, how lame the entire plan had been. I envisioned a well-structured session with a touch, maybe more than a touch, of spite toward Faye Marin and her pseudo science. A lark, with my favorite patient. We—I—completely screwed up.

"Wake up. Sounds easy enough," Wong said.

He rattled out the phrase to a suspicious Amy. She emitted another stream of fluent Asiatic, causing him to step backward in surprise.

"She just reamed me out in what sounds like Mandarin and started talking in Japanese, and about all I know in that is the song, 'Linda Linda.'"

After another rush of syllables, she leaned back on her heels, clearly considering us ignorant beyond words.

Not her father's Indian dialect, apparently. A torrent of questions dogged my mind, but first things first. We were beginning to draw onlookers, and since a simple command in any language appeared unlikely to resolve the situation, I would have to call out Brackenridge Hospital's psych unit to bring her in.

What a screw-up, I murmured to myself while pulling out my phone. The hospital operator connected me almost immediately to the unit's staff psychiatrist. Too polite to remark on the peculiarity of the situation, she promised a unit there in less than ten minutes.

Mike wrenched the phone out of my hand. "I need that, Carla. I'm setting up a conference call with Toni Akugawa."

"We can consult with her later."

"She speaks Japanese. Her parents made an effort to use it at home, and she spent a summer over there. Here we go."

He thrust the phone back in my hand.

Dr. Akugawa's voice sounded annoyingly perky. "It sounds like you're having way too much excitement tonight."

"Dr. Akugawa, he handed my phone back to me. I need you to tell my patient that everything's... no, find out from her what she thinks is happening, how old she is."

"Does she think she is a child?"

"Perhaps. We're not quite sure what happened during the session, whether she's cycling through early childhood vestigial memories—"

"Or is projecting a previously hidden persona," Mike added from his phone.

I knocked that ball off the court. "Dissociative identity disorder's extremely rare and would have surfaced long before now, given the challenges she's faced in the past few years."

"Doctors," Dr. Akugawa interjected. "Let me talk to her. Her name is Amy what?"

"Duran."

Mike reached over and tossed the tiny phone into her lap, where it rested for a moment. With great care, she examined its back. When she delicately turned it over, she grunted her surprise at the panel display.

"Look!"

Having gotten her attention, I stepped closer and mimed how to use the phone.

She pressed it against her ear and said forcefully, "Moshi-moshi."

Bringing my phone to my ear, I heard Dr. Akugawa say, "Dr. Turner, she just said hello. I'll ask her a few questions."

The few questions stretched into a lengthy conversation as Amy, her face as animated as her voice, seemed desperate to communicate with Dr. Akugawa.

The bystanders, their view largely blocked off by Rashida's crew, began to drift away.

"Mama?" Rashida hovered nearby.

I put my hand up just as Dr. Akugawa managed to dam the flood of words.

"Whew. Dr. Turner, you have yourself a very sticky situation. Ms. Duran isn't there anymore. This man, who by the way speaks Japanese like a native, *lots* better than me, he's never heard of her, and he wants to know the way back to his neighborhood."

"What?"

"Since the Olympics are going on, there are quite a few foreigners in town. He thinks maybe he's in a special housing area built for them, but he's totally lost."

"He? She thinks she's a Japanese male?"

"His name's Isao Watanabe. He's forty-two years old, it's 1964, and until several years ago, he'd been a *salariman* designing ads for Takeshita Electronics. Since then, he's been an actor. Dr. Turner, this sounds as though your patient created an elaborate fantasy world and has now decided to live there as this persona."

"Hold on."

I told Mike the news. As we were deciding what to do, the crisis team from Brackenridge showed up, looking sharp in their dark blue scrubs and carrying rolled-up restraints.

I asked them to step back a bit and got back on the phone. How disorienting, to hear her voice on the phone blasting away in an alien tongue, doing the same in person a few feet away. It created a doubling effect, real and unreal at the same time, as all the while perspiration trickled down my back and laughter rang out from Esther's Follies.

Feeling the need to create another identity, Amy kept it hidden through our years of exploring her emotional landscape. An amazing, inexplicable achievement.

Dr. Akugawa managed to surface.

"Mr. Watanabe demands to go back to his apartment. He also wants you people to return his clothes, thank you very much, and while you're at it, tell him how long he's been in a coma. He badly needs a haircut. He also wants to know what kind of drugs you have given him, because he's hallucinating bodily features he refuses to discuss. Dr. Turner, your patient's in meltdown."

A patient, in acute dissociation from her body, from her surroundings, from her very life. A patient, exhibiting schizoid symptoms that may or not actually be schizophrenia. She might be in a fugue state, caused by a trance-suggested mimicking of dissociative identity disorder or DID. For the moment, she may believe that she has multiple personalities. What role did the beta-anodynol play, if any?

"Dr. Akugawa, tell her that she's not well and that we're trying to take care of her if she'll let us. Tell her we want to take her to the hospital where we hope to answer all her questions."

The conversation went on for a while until finally Dr. Akugawa broke into English.

"Okay, Dr. Turner, I'm on my way to Brackenridge. I told him I'd met him there. He doesn't trust you or Mike, but he'll give you thirty minutes to correct the situation. In the meantime, I would suggest kid gloves. This guy served in the war, the big one, and I don't think he trusts *gaijin*."

"Guy what?"

"*Gaijin*. Foreigners. I'm walking out my door right now. I'll talk him into your car so you can drive him over to the hospital. Don't grab his arm or try to force him. We might get through this without any bruises."

Amy rose to her feet, exhausted yet brooking no invasion of her territory. Mike gestured that we wanted to take her on a drive.

Before we did that, Rashida said goodbye to Mike with a wave. She gave me a quick hug after I promised a full explanation when I got home. "And don't tell Imani anything about this when you go pick her up."

Amy regarded the sidewalk, passers-by, my Toyota Avalon, everything with the same thousand-yard stare. I might possibly get home before dawn. Amy, on the other hand, appeared destined for a longer stay, despite her demand for a thirty-minute cure.

I still needed to call her brother.

F I V E

"I HOPE THE FOOD SUITED YOU," THE YOUNG MAN WITH BRILLIANT RED HAIR SAID anxiously.

Isao studied the mounded remains of his breakfast. Heavily spiced fried meat, salty eggs, toasted bread, milk, strong hot tea, and a delicious cup of sliced fruit. It was a huge meal, as though he expected to hike up Mount Fuji. At least the fog in his mind had lifted.

The gaijin, Ben was his name, placed chopsticks on the table beside the bed.

"I pray I promptly could have found this promptly, honorable sir miss, assisting I you in your enjoying. Anything else I to procure—you require?"

"Coffee, if you have it."

He seemed surprised. "Yes, speedy to the nurse I will talk upon your requiring."

A Japanese woman, with an accent no better than the gaijin but with better grammar, had already been by to explain how Isao came to be in a foreigners' hospital and in a foreigner's body. She told a ridiculous tale set in the next century, composed of lies he immediately rejected.

He initially believed that scientists kidnapped him for a bizarre operation, but a careful exploration of the body revealed no stitches on the head or below. Although frail in appearance, the body felt strong.

He guessed that he should say her body, but after all, he was using it, wasn't he? So shouldn't he claim it as his own? Too confusing. With any luck, there wouldn't be another trip to the toilet for a few hours. Gods, what a strange experience. The shiny white porcelain almost blinded him.

"Where is this place?" he asked again, hoping for a different answer.

"Austin, Texas, America, honorable miss sir. Many computer factories in Austin.

Many musicians in Austin. Big university in Austin. We are a big city but we are not a big city to beauteous Tokyo. We are small big."

Ben worked his hands to demonstrate, as though Isao were a child in a classroom. Many computer factories and a big university added up to numerous men wearing lab coats. This accounted for why they did the surgery in a town he had never heard of rather than New York City. New York City. If he were crazy or the victim of mad scientists, why couldn't it have been there. They might have let him out to see a play.

That truck horn he heard... he must have been struck by one of those idiot drivers and then shipped off to America. American doctors could fix anything, but why use a woman's body? For that matter, how did that grinning doctor and his African assistant fit into what happened?

"Do you enjoying sporting games, hobbies, enjoying studies?" Beads of perspiration formed on the man's wide forehead.

"Baseball, movies, and I used to take tango lessons."

"Baseball is good. I am enjoying baseball also like you."

The gaijin spoke enthusiastically, picking up a small plastic rectangle with buttons. He pointed at the television, which came on immediately. Channels flashed by quickly before he stopped on a station.

"This one is showing many games, and will have one for your enjoying."

The set had a beautiful color picture, which meant, first off, that the hospital considered him to be important patient, as he doubted even in America color televisions were rolled out for just anybody, and secondly, that... Isao stared at the screen, dumbfounded, at the close-up of the baseball player.

"Kimura, yes," Ben said. "Most good player. The new Ichiro. The Yankees think he is most good."

A more Japanese face could not be found. The camera moved out some distance to show Kimura stepping into a dugout where a line of players pounded on his back. Kimura must have scored a run. For the Yankees. A Japanese player in America. And not the first one, if there was an old Ichiro.

Once Ben figured out he needed to shut up, they watched the game together in a silence broken only by Isao's gasps during commercials. Drivers in futuristic cars, bony women dressed in provocative clothing, splashy signs that blew up or flew off in different directions, products he couldn't begin to guess the uses for—he could not keep up with the images, they went by so frenetically.

He laid back and stared at the ceiling. He paid no attention to Ben, who, after turning off the television, left with a well-spoken goodbye.

You should be dead, Isao thought to himself. Dead and reduced to ashes long ago, leaving behind a widow who probably married her bastard lover and a son who forgot he ever had a father.

"Why am I here?" he asked aloud.

IN THE NOW

THE SCENE AT THE AIRPORT WAS UNEXPECTEDLY EMOTIONAL BECAUSE ALTHOUGH Imani hated it when she displayed any signs of so-called childishness, she was, after all, going on her first plane ride alone and would be gone most of the summer.

She gave me a chokehold of a hug, her wiry arms weight-room strong, then kissed me on the cheek and told me not to work too hard. Little chance of that happening. I managed to say something about hoping she enjoyed her summer, to remember that I loved her, and to listen to her grandparents. It had been a trying night, so no wonder I felt shaky.

Her eyes widened at the sight of her mother losing it.

"I love you, too, and I'll make you proud."

As per my request, Rashida didn't explain to her friends why Amy ended up on Sixth Street, which left my daughter full to bursting to share her theory with me, now that we had sent Imani off to Tennessee. According to Rashida, when we gave Amy the beta-whatchamawhoozie, Amy's spirit somehow became detached from her body, and the ghost of a Japanese man who died somewhere in the area took over the body.

Amy's spirit needed to get back in, but was lost. Regarding why the ghost couldn't speak English, broken or otherwise, Rashida said the answer was obvious. The ghost was remembering when he was young and living back home in Japan, not when he was older and had immigrated to a foreign country. Our only course of action had to be to give the drug again, tell the ghost that he was in the wrong body, and wait for Amy.

"You have to do it back at your office," Rashida finished triumphantly. "That way, Miss Duran can find her way back."

I was too tired to set her straight and decided to save it for later. It troubled me that after well over twelve years of quality education and an upbringing free of Faye Marin-style pop voodoo, Rashida picked the least likely explanation for last night's events.

Ghosts. In a matter of speaking, ghosts inhabit us all, each phase in our life represented by the child who wet her pants, the teenager who felt awkward at school dances, and adult misadventures.

All the people we once were still influencing our current and future actions. But to say that they are discorporate beings or separate personalities, as Mike seemed to be advocating, violated both common sense and professional logic.

I dropped Rashida off and headed back to the hospital.

Amy sat on the side of her bed, dressed in a faded blue hospital gown that failed to disguise her thin, yet well-conditioned legs. No wonder she'd been able to lead us on such a chase. High cheekbones set off her lucid brown eyes, eyes that gazed at us intently. The wariness of last night had faded but little.

Toni tapped an audio recorder on the bedside table.

"I'll have this translated by a service. You'll get it by e-mail the second I receive it. Ms. Duran's friend is in the waiting room wanting to talk to you. Mike's bringing in a man from Borlauch who's native-born Japanese. He's also familiar with the med you used. I'm with you about that, however. I don't see how it has any bearing on what we do from here on out."

A white woman with long, reddish-blonde hair, Nina came into the room and informed me in no uncertain terms that Amy did not belong in an institution.

"You may be correct," I told her. "But right now, she doesn't think she's Amy, and until we're certain that she won't try to run away again, she needs to stay here."

That seemed to satisfy her. Although she gladly answered my questions about Amy, she could shed no light on the Japan obsession.

Amy never expressed the slightest interest in anything Asian. She was also at ease in both orientation and gender, Nina quickly pointed out before I could pose the question.

"Whatever's going on with Amy, it's not because she wants to be a dude."

Nina worked as a singer-bassist and supplemented her income by giving lessons. She had attended college with Amy and remained close friends with her through the years. Amy took no trips to Japan, dated no Japanese women, never even used chopsticks at Asian restaurants.

"Randall's checking out her attic, the shed out back, and the garage," Nina said. "He's trying to find something for you."

I brought up the subject of Amy's finances, which provoked a nervous spasm of laughter from Nina. She volunteered that Amy kept ironclad control over her budget, to the point of allocating precise amounts to spend on presents.

She thought Gordon was rolling in money. He was an investments wizard who recently began a second career that somehow combined photography and making art deals. His son, Randall, was the product of an early failed marriage that landed Gordon with sole custody.

When I came back to the observation room, Mike had arrived from the airport with his hired guns—a slender, mellow-faced Japanese man who appeared to be in his late thirties, and an older, petite white woman with sharp features. Dr. Jiro Endo and Lisa Gillespie, both eager to see Amy.

When they walked into the room, Amy leaped to her feet and bowed to the man, exhaling what looked like a greeting. From the corner of my eye, I saw Toni turn her recorder back on. I stepped back closer to the door, almost bumping into

Nina.

"Amy," Nina called out confidently.

Everyone, including Amy, turned their heads toward her. The heat in her friend's eyes, alien and searching, caused Nina to gasp audibly. I turned around to see Nina rushing down the hall.

When I returned my attention to the room, I realized the interrogation in Japanese had already begun.

Dr. Endo rifled questions at Amy with lightning speed while Gillespie stood close by with her own recorder.

Toni came over to me and whispered, "This is the real stuff. I can barely make sense of it. It's like he's deliberately mixing up slang and specialized terms, throwing everything at her to trip her up. To be honest, it's beyond me."

"Then what are we doing here?" I whispered back.

She had no answer, but I had one. Mike and his people's apparent agenda consisted of framing Amy as a fraud. I had to be her advocate, even if she hadn't a clue that she needed one.

Amy's confidence didn't flag during the interrogation. Her gestures became at turns graceful and elongated, or abrupt and physical. Boldly confident, so unlike her normal timid bearing. Suddenly, she got to her feet and marched up and down beside the bed, chanting something—perhaps a cadence—then she broke into song with a clear, tuneful alto.

"I'll be damned," I heard Gordon mumble behind me. "When did she learn to sing?"

Both he and Randall seemed close to the breaking point, so I took them down to the cafeteria for breakfast. Over eggs and bacon, they told me how much Amy loved music, despite being unable to carry a tune, and that she still practiced the violin.

The everyday minutia I learned about Amy reminded me of why I had come to care for her. She probably would have driven me crazy with the perfection of her housekeeping and her pristine garden—hard to live up to such standards— but the Amy who sang off-key, who rooted for her favorite teams, that was an Amy I wish I had known first-hand.

The Durans could have hidden the evidence of Amy's self-education in all things Japanese, but neither of them appeared to be faking the emotion of their reactions.

Possibly, she checked books out of the library and kept them hidden from visitors at home. Just then, I received a text message from Toni. They had finished the interview.

Except for the Durans, who decided to follow the library angle by going over to question staffers at the branch Amy frequented, everyone sat soberly around the meeting room table waiting for Dr. Endo to begin. Toni had already sent a courier from the translation service scurrying with the request for a rapid transcript.

Looking wan, Dr. Endo took out a handkerchief and wiped his face. "I want to thank you for letting me know so quickly about what happened here."

I'd expected a thick Japanese accent, but Endo's first words in English came out with more of a Great Lakes cadence, mildly layered with his origins.

"Watanabe was able to fill me in a lot of things—when he was born, his family, where he attended school, his military service, and his marriage. Plus, he had a lot of questions for me. I only wish I could have answered them."

"Excuse me, Jiro." Gillespie's face was skeptical. "She came prepared for anything you could throw at her. Any question she asks is just her blowing smoke. She knows we're on to her."

"Excuse me, Lisa, for not making myself clear." Endo didn't bother to shade the sarcasm. "The patient in that hospital room's a man. A man. He carries himself like a Japanese male, but old school, like my grandfather. My mom and I moved to Toronto when I was a teenager, but I remember how he was. Watanabe, he's light on his feet, like he's never stepped on a crack, but at the same time, you know he'd finish any fight I was stupid enough to start. He has an old-fashioned way of speaking, but not like in a samurai movie. I don't know how to explain it."

"It's called acting; that's how you explain it," Gillespie snapped. "Besides, Zilinsky said that she's a lesbian."

"Your point being?" I kept my eyes on Mike, who looked embarrassed.

"She asked," Mike said defensively. "I told her"—he turned to Gillespie—"I told you, Lisa, that Ms. Duran didn't act masculine before the session. And even if she did, I don't see how it'd matter."

I knew he'd said his last words for my benefit, but I appreciated them, anyway.

"It matters because it speaks to her ability to pretend." Gillespie wasn't a mere company flack, not with that hard-skull, imperious attitude. Dr. Nyanga sent down a verbal enforcer. "They have to lie at first, don't they? As far as her acting dykey, don't you think she'd be experienced from being around those types?"

In the interest of professionalism, I decided not to respond to Gillespie's idiocy.

Jiro Endo shrugged his shoulders. "Maybe you've got a Meryl Streep on your hands, but I don't think even Streep could make you think she's a man without doing something with makeup. It's not studying them in person or watching every Japanese movie ever made. He's not trying to impress me or get one over on me. He's tired, he's pissed, and he wants to go home."

He stopped to wipe his face again, appearing overwhelmed. "I asked him about Ms. Duran. He doesn't know where she's gone. Watanabe doesn't know her."

"What's his explanation for what happened?" I asked.

"The last thing he remembers is being upset over his wife sleeping with another man. He remembers walking into a busy street. He believes that he's a ghost." Rashida's theory. "He has no idea how he got here."

"Great." Mike's face exactly mirrored Gillespie's, each in the throes of acute discomfort. "Our message to Dr. Nyanga is that beta-anodynol has an unusual side-effect: it causes traveling ghost syndrome. What's the cure?"

Though the question was sarcastic, Endo pondered it for a moment.

"I don't know that he's a ghost, but he is real."

S I X

THAT EVENING, MIKE AND THE HIRED GUNS FLEW BACK TO CHICAGO. THE NEXT FEW days settled into an uneasy routine in which Toni Akugawa and I, both juggling around our regular clients, took turns working with Amy. They had moved her into a room on the psych floor, one with less of a prison ambience.

For my sessions, I relied on a translator on retainer from Brackenridge. Ben Stovall seemed unfazed by the novelty of dealing with a ghost. A ghost fascinated by American television.

Television, he told me by way of Stovall, convinced him that he was not *baka yaro,* a crazy fool, nor had rogue American scientists kidnapped him. Even Hollywood couldn't afford that many special effects in its programming.

Stovall remarked to me one day, "This is like *Quantum Leap.*"

"Pardon?"

"Some show I've seen on cable. A man travels through the past and spends time in other people's bodies."

"Where are the original owners?"

"I dunno. What I can't figure out is how Isao jumped into the future and why into Miss Duran's body. It doesn't make sense."

He shook his head mournfully as Isao looked back and forth at each of us, trying to divine the subject matter.

This alternate persona acted self-assured despite the circumstance. His habitual politeness might have met the national stereotype, and his eyes kept darting away from meeting mine, but I saw what Dr. Jiro Endo was talking about. Isao didn't swagger when he walked. He fully occupied his space. One might say that he owned it. Call it the masculine imperative.

It took him a couple of sessions to quit asking for Mike—he initially saw me as a subordinate he needed to get past. His appraisal of my physical attributes came in sideways glances, but again, he didn't push it.

Amy remained throughout our acquaintance a buttoned-down personality. She'd subtly expressed her attraction to me.

Isao fulfilled certain needs for her that had remained undisclosed during years of therapy. Although I thought I knew her well, she had kept this secret hidden from me.

I reluctantly agreed with Mike that Amy might have dissociative identity disorder, or a related condition, for Isao had emerged during hypnosis. This was a common enough occurrence in the medical literature concerning DID, and to me, a likely sign that the patient was attempting to please those conducting a session. Amy's situation, however, went far beyond cooked-up cases and eager patients seeking an out from confronting their problems.

According to the literature, alternates might vary in gender, age and emotional type, but all were legitimate spin-offs from the patient's baseline. What accounted for Isao in her emotional life that she needed to be a Japanese man, and a long-dead veteran at that?

I watched the session recording repeatedly, unable to find hidden cues in the recording, nothing that encouraged Isao to declare dominance over Amy.

Counter-suggestion, a technique I'd used before with over-dramatizing clients, had a serious drawback for this case. I could tell Isao he was making excellent progress, but would Amy get the message?

Amy had disappeared, leaving behind a forty-two-year-old Japanese man in her wake. The baseball-loving former adman had become friendlier in the weeks since his admission, but this construct of Amy's imagination wouldn't relinquish control to his owner.

Phone calls and a visit to her boss and coworkers at Bookish revealed a dedicated, perfectionist employee, who came off as more straight-laced than her coworkers did, but with a caring side. I didn't reveal anything about her case, other than she had experienced a strong reaction to a medication.

No one could recall her ever having an interest in Japanese literature. Amy was an assistant manager with Next Boss written all over her, as one woman put it. To judge from their reactions, however, her coworkers liked her. Her boss assured me that he had been chanting every morning for Amy's good health.

This was a prayer later echoed by her rabbi, a beefy man named Fleischer. I couldn't see what harm it would do for him to visit with Isao, who displayed a cautious curiosity about Amy. But, once again, the radical disconnect between her appearance and behavior stunned the visitor into silence.

"Well," Rabbi Fleischer finally said. "Have you seen Amy?"

Ben translated both ways.

"Okay, he's seen pictures of her but so far, no, he hasn't come across her yet. He's sorry he, uh, came here because he knows that people must be worried about her. He doesn't know the way back."

We collected considerable information about Isao from the transcripts and from notes Toni and I, via Ben, collected. Isao was born in 1922 in Tokyo to a prosperous internist and his wife, a noted beauty. He had an older brother, Koichii, and a younger sister, Kaoru.

He stood a scant five-foot-three, with brown eyes, black hair, and weak eyesight. He still had mortar fragments lodged in his right knee.

After he graduated from senior school in 1940, he entered the Army where he made a rough adjustment to military discipline. He almost ended up in the stockade over an incident involving a drill instructor.

"He kept slapping the recruits around, trying to shake us up. Those who couldn't handle it got slapped even harder. He kept asking us why we thought he was slapping us, and none of the answers we gave was right. Slap, slap, slap."

Isao thwacked the side of his chair for emphasis. "The drill instructor said the only answer was 'I do not know.' He told us that we needed only to obey what we were told."

Grinning now, Isao continued.

"So I started humming the soldier's song. The part where it says 'I shall die only for the Emperor; I shall never look back.' The drill instructor knocked me down but later he said I had a fine voice and would make a good soldier once I grew up some."

A decorated soldier captured when the Allies retook the Philippines, Isao spent some time in a Dutch-administered prisoner of war camp before being shipped back home.

He married the youngest daughter of a famed No actor, fathered a son, and worked at a large zaibatsu for several years. At that point, he did something unthinkable for a man of his generation—he quit and became an actor.

Humming a snippet of the soldier's tune, Isao bounced from his chair to a perch on the windowsill, the barred window behind him. He clearly wanted to be elsewhere, that elsewhere being Tokyo circa 1964, where he owned tickets to several Olympic events, including Bob Hayes's then-Olympic record in the 100-meter dash.

One day, I noticed a piece of artwork tacked on the wall by the nurses' station. Isao had drawn a delicate ink portrait of Ben Stovall, who spent many of his off-hours with my client. Along the side ran a descending line of Japanese characters. Yet another talent never mentioned by Amy.

Ben explained that Isao had given the portrait in appreciation of their humane concern. The characters were a traditional wish for good fortune.

Isao displayed no signs of mental confusion and seemed in good spirits. According to the charge nurse, the staff kept confusing the names in their patient notes. Amy was no more than a theory to them, Isao the reality.

The nurse mentioned an incident where a staff member noticed that Isao had been in the bathroom for quite some time. She bolted into the bathroom only to find that Isao had stuffed towels into the crack under the door and run hot water to try to create a Japanese-style steam bath.

Where was Amy hiding in this man? Did he represent a sublimated desire for gender reassignment? If so, Gordon reported no episodes of gender confusion in her childhood.

At first, Toni and I fought hard with the Durans to approve medications we thought might help. The discussion went no further than that, since Gordon refused to consider any drug for his sister other than for normal complaints.

This left us facing a long-term care situation, one that Brackenridge wasn't set up for, and neither of us welcomed the prospect of placing our patient into an extended care residential-type setting, that is, if we could even find a space on such short notice.

The only other options were the state hospital or outpatient care, and we knew how Gordon would react to the first possibility. We both felt uneasy about approving outpatient status.

"What if she spontaneously begins conversion to some other personality we haven't encountered yet?" I said. "What if she leaves town, even flees to Japan? We can't risk losing track of her."

"You know, Carla, Isao's a fully functional personality," Toni said. "I know our goal is to get Ms. Duran back, but let's not lose sight of the fact that we have to enlist Isao in this process. We co-opt him, we weaken him, and we eliminate him."

Gordon and Randall's own efforts at reaching Amy, carefully mediated by both Toni and me, had also failed. Although he understood that these were Amy's relatives and tried to please them, the effort left all three emotionally drained.

From then on, whenever one or both of the Durans visited daily, they talked, via Ben, about superficial topics. Hard to discern whether they'd formed a connection, when Isao had to know that the Durans wanted him gone.

A few days after the fact, Randall reported that he had moved into Amy's house, hoping to prevent another break-in.

"They didn't do much. Broke in through the back door, ate some of her food, played games on her computer, messed up the papers in her study. Probably some dumbass in the neighborhood who knew she hadn't been home in a while. Dad put double locks on the doors and I'm sleeping there at nights, which is kind of nice.

"I take care of her plants and I keep the yard looking pretty good. You probably think I'm being stupid but sometimes I like pretending she's out shopping. Any minute now, she'll come in all loaded down and wanting me to bring in the rest of the bags."

He fought to control his emotions. "You've got to get her back."

I WAS LEAVING MY OFFICE ONE DAY WHEN A VOICE STOPPED ME.

"Dr. Turner?"

I turned around and saw Nina, her eyes red-rimmed and hair disheveled. For however long, she'd been waiting outside my office.

"I'm sorry to bother you like this," she said.

"It's no bother at all. We can go back inside if you'd like."

"No, no. Gordon says you think it's some kind of delusion or Sybil thing going on, but that's dead wrong. Do you know how much Amy liked you? I'm betting you liked her, too. That's why you're so gung-ho to find a psych excuse for what's happened, but you can't do it the way you're going. You've got to look elsewhere—and don't ask me where. All I know is Amy isn't freaking crazy. You've got to find her. Please."

SEVEN

During dinner, Ethiopian cuisine by way of Central Market, I half-listened to Rashida's account of her morning duel in Comparative European Lit class with a snotty graduate assistant. Charles White's painting over the crystal hutch drew my attention.

The painting depicted two women at a produce market, picking through bruised vegetables and carrying on a conversation. Sometimes I pretended the chat to be about rambunctious children or nosy neighbors. Tonight they seemed to be talking about how unsettled they felt in their early 1960s world of protests and rising black consciousness.

Rashida looked at me, her face pensive.

"Mama, you can talk to me about it. You've been good about not bringing work home, but maybe you should sometimes. I'm old enough to deal with what's going on."

So I told her all of it, including the fact that I cared for Amy and, according to Nina, Amy had felt much the same about me. How thus far nothing had worked to bring her back. A crushing weight lifted from my body, a burden I only then realized I had been carrying.

Before she died, Belle gave me permission to date again. To fall in love, if it came to that. Overwhelmed by the thought of her dying, I couldn't conceive of my life after her passing. Since the girls had been four and one, respectively, when Belle and I became partners, they had spent their lives with me as their co-parent, and the past several years as their widowed mother. Belle understood better than I did about the passage of time. How the pain never fades yet the need for love persists.

Over my protests, Belle spoke to me from her hospice bed about being receptive to change, or as she put it, "Baby, you're not built for widow's black. Move on. Find a place for your love. Otherwise, you'll go bats."

I realized with a start that Rashida was talking.

"I was just trippin' the other day, talking about ghosts, but I've been thinking what if you've done what you set out to do? What if Amy went back and saw her past life and something got messed up to where they ended up changing places."

The thought had occurred to me. I kicked into a corner where it belonged.

"'Shida, there can't be any such thing as reincarnation or karma."

"But what if there is something to it? Just 'cause I haven't found him on the Net doesn't mean anything. I can't read Japanese."

I'd made my own tour of the Internet late one night, curious about how Amy invented Isao Watanabe, but came up against the same problem as Rashida. Although several men used his name on social networking sites, the current bearers had no resemblance to Amy's veteran/actor.

I couldn't think of anything to say to my daughter. It was like the law of gravity to her: until the ball landed on her foot, it literally wouldn't make an impression. I couldn't disprove Isao to her until we'd made more progress in Amy's treatment. That ball was still in the air.

I tore off another piece of injera and returned to eating.

Toni Akugawa and I met in my office to discuss Amy's case with Mike via Skype.

Before I could begin my report, Mike interrupted me with an emphatic curse.

"There's no point in this, Carla. You aren't going to get anywhere talking to him. We have to go back and give the beta-anodynol again, do the induction, every last bit of it."

Toni quickly agreed, but again, Mike interrupted me before I could raise an objection.

"We've checked him out thoroughly. Our people in Japan scraped up everything they could find. Did you know he served in the Philippines, Carla?"

Which explained Isao's reticence about the war years.

"Amy based her alternate on a real person?" I said.

"Check this out."

He looked down for a moment. A black and white photograph came onscreen, that of a good-looking Japanese man shot in a movie star pose. Isao possessed a heart-shaped, delicate face, with mischievous eyes.

Mike came back on screen.

"We have copies of photographs from plays he appeared in. All contemporary—for the 1960s, that is—and not a kimono in the bunch. I'll send you the jpegs, pdfs, and everything else we found. I also have pictures of his widow, who's been dead for decades. After Isao died, she married a TV producer of those Astroboy knockoffs in the '70s. And we've tracked down Isao's son, Masao Watanabe. He's living in Seattle, of all places. He's retired from the diplomatic corps. His son, Isao's grandson, is in the same line of work for the Japanese consulate there."

"How did Amy dig up information about this man?" I asked.

"It's plausible that she came up with all this on her own, but there's absolutely no evidence she did. Isao's son and grandson have been in Seattle less than six months. The son was never more than middle echelon, and the grandson hasn't risen high enough in the ranks to generate more than an occasional press release. We can't prove a path that shows Amy latched on to Isao by way of them, or vice-versa. The fact that they're in the States is interesting, but diplomacy's like acting. In a way, Masao took after his father."

The break-in at Amy's house. It finally hit me what had happened. Borlauch authorized a burglary, perhaps by Gillespie, who struck me as being an operative. Mike never returned his key to my office, but no point in changing the lock now.

I had to assume that Borlauch's spooks did a thorough investigation, including phone traces and financial transactions. If Gordon launched a lawsuit, the case wouldn't simply lay out how Mike and I screwed up that night. A drug that eliminated addictive behavior also removed the need for punishment and excuses. That posed a complicated enough challenge for puritans and hedonists alike. A drug that produced past lives, however, affronted core Western beliefs. The majority of Borlauch's shareholders held such beliefs, most likely.

Mike was lucky still to be on his company's payroll. To judge from his appearance, face drawn and voice shot through with fatigue, he knew his job was on shaky ground.

"So, what are you saying, Mike, that Nyanga has you chasing after a ghost?" Toni sounded skeptical.

"Or that Isao isn't a ghost at all."

I echoed my daughter's words from last night. I felt the unreality of the situation sinking into my bones. It had been my last hope, that Borlauch would uncover a conspiracy or some previously unknown Japanese connection. It would save me from having to consider the unthinkable.

Toni stopped tapping into her laptop and glanced over at me, her eyebrows raised.

"I've never ever heard of this scenario. They don't switch places; the old life never sticks around. How could it? The past is past, Mike," Toni said.

It turned out that Mike had been spending a great deal of his time researching reincarnation. He paid a visit to an expert on Buddhism, and he talked to Faye Marin. Hearing that name sent me off in a rant that the others allowed me to indulge in for far too long.

Realizing how petty I sounded, I shut up and raised my hand, as if to ask for a time-out.

"I know, I know," Mike said. "Someone at Borlauch got wind of why we'd been recording it, and they went right to her with the story. The leak could be from one of her true believers, but I think it might be someone who wants to make Dr. Nyanga look bad. Internal politics. Marin's agreed to keep quiet if Borlauch gives her an exclusive when they do release the story. Although I think they'll want to stall her indefinitely. Nyanga's insisting on keeping all the participants anonymous, so there's one break."

He waved his hand dismissively. "Anyway, back to what I was saying: the Buddhist expert's never heard of anything remotely like it. Karma can't work if your past life joins you in the present. You don't learn your lessons. You're throwing cause and effect in the same blender. It can't be done, he said. Okay, it's as though you were a child abuser in your last life and had to pay for it by being abused in your current life. Throwing your two lives together breaks the rules, and it would make your next life after that a frigging mess. His theory is that when we gave the patient the beta-anodynol, we polluted the stream, which allowed another spirit to enter her body. Marin pretty much thinks the same thing—that Watanabe's a wandering spirit."

"A ghost, in other words, and not a past life. I can't believe we have to deal with Marin."

I couldn't remove the disgust from my voice.

"I don't know if she's any more wrong than we are," Toni said flatly. "I think all our theories are flawed, including my own, but I'm not about to get dragged into debating spirits versus past lives."

Reluctantly, and with a sour fatalism, I agreed to arrange a beta-anodynol session with Amy/Isao, this time in a surgical chamber with an observation gallery, which offered the best hope for limiting spectators.

———

"WHY DO YOU THINK YOU CAME HERE?" BEN STOVALL ASKED ONE EVENING IN the communal room.

The Yankees pulled out a tenth-inning rally thanks to a sacrifice fly by Kimura. The friends were enjoying a round of Coca-Colas as the other patients, who seemed more sad than crazy, gradually returned to their rooms.

"Why did I come back? To watch baseball games in color."

He added a laugh since Ben sometimes couldn't tell when Isao was making a joke.

Ben always kept a smile on his face, even when asking a serious question. Spending the evening with him had been fun. Ben even tried to talk the charge nurse into allowing them to go for a drive around town, but Isao backed out of the plan.

He felt safer in the hospital, around people who called him by his name and didn't seem to mind if sometimes he hid in his room and stared at the wall. Early on, a nurse gave him a Bible written in Japanese. He dumped it in a drawer after she left.

If heaven did exist, Isao had no intention of ending up in whatever they had over Texas. Although he had come to appreciate Ben, he couldn't imagine spending eternity around nothing but gaijins.

Ben looked at him expectantly.

"Why I am here. I'm here because of a mistake. I don't know what caused the mistake, but the doctors are trying to fix it."

"A place is there they can keep you here, and find there a place for that woman going?" Be asked.

Ben was doing better on speaking and understanding Japanese than when they first met, but there were still times Isao had to keep his reactions in check. What a weird accent.

Did Ben mean, could Isao stay somewhere else when the Duran woman returned?

"I don't see how. This is her body, not mine."

Ben's eyes brimmed over with tears. "You can stay with me."

How to explain so Ben could understand it.

"I'm not supposed to be here. When I'm gone, everything will be back in place. I thought I'd die in the war, but I didn't. Maybe it's hard to kill me," he said with a small laugh, but Ben didn't join in.

Isao wasn't sure why he didn't feel as upset as Ben about the situation. Maybe because Isao didn't believe it was really happening. As long as he felt that way, it didn't matter what the doctors did. He would exist in this body, take care of its needs, and soon, hopefully very soon, give it back to the woman.

THAT EVENING, I WENT OVER TO VISIT GORDON AT AMY'S HOUSE, WHERE HE AND Randall were busy doing some touch-up work on her yard. Hardly any weeds had grown during her absence, which Gordon took to be a sign of her excellent gardening skills. Or her religious use of Weed-and-Feed.

A fine mist rose from the sprinkler. We sat on her porch and drank iced tea, wrapped in the fragrance from her roses. We talked about not much in particular until, with reluctance, I brought up the session, planned in two days.

As he listened, Randall said under his breath, "I knew it, I knew it," but his father, far more somber, kept his counsel until the end.

In his deep growl, Gordon rambled on about how peculiar it seemed to him that people who went through regression usually could only speak their native tongue.

"They claim that you're remembering the experience and reporting it back to the questioner. About that channeling fan you mentioned, it looks awful convenient that they're tuning in ancient spirits who use English."

Randall broke in long enough to mention a reported case of a past life speaking a language foreign to the host.

Gordon's laugh had a bitter tinge.

"Put it on TV, get it investigated, prove it. They can't. If it happened once in an ashram, then it can be repeated in a lab. That's why I never believed in it. I don't know how her past life got here. I don't have the slightest idea how he switched with her. He does seem like a nice person, but hell, so is Amy. Why wouldn't he be a good guy?

"He needs to go wherever it is he needs to go. To the grave, if that's how it works. Or if we all have our past lives tucked away in a mental file cabinet, then he needs to go crawl in there and let Amy get on with her business. I want my sister back."

N I N E

"DR. TURNER, DR. TURNER," A VOICE CALLED OUT TO ME AT THE ELEVATOR entrance.

Stopping to turn around, I held back the door, only then realizing that Dr. Jiro Endo had come back to town without Lisa Gillespie, the Borlauch operative.

Everything was set up for the session with only the principles needed there. Toni Akugawa, Ben Stovall, and Isao were on their way down to the operating arena.

With much to lose or gain with the results of the session, Borlauch couldn't risk the possibility of unfiltered news leaking out to the media. Borlauch and the hospital administration were enforcing a publicity blackout that included signed agreements from everyone involved to keep their collective mouths shut.

Dr. Nyanga, the research head, was present, along with a sprinkling of other Borlauch potentates, plus Faye Marin.

Rashida flatly stated over breakfast that she would be there, no matter what.

Endo stood next to me in the elevator quietly until he spoke in a feathery voice as we exited the elevator.

"I want to translate for the session. I want to be there."

Something about the emotion in his face got to me. Resting my hand on his shoulder, I asked what he thought would happen.

He looked at me, almost smiling. "A miracle... and please call me Jiro."

"Jiro, do you think you're going to have proof for reincarnation? Is that what you're expecting?"

"Isao shouldn't have come back the way he did. And to have stayed this long?

This isn't proof the way I grew up believing. I expected to find a liar, and then I thought I'd met a ghost. But now? It's like I see my grandfather in Isao's eyes. I'm here for him but I also want to help bring back your Amy."

How did he know of my affection for Amy? Was it that obvious in our previous discussions?

No one with a half a brain should trust a Borlauch man. In which case, I was ignorance personified, for I agreed that Isao needed a native speaker to interpret for him. Ben went upstairs to help translate for the observers.

The actual reunion with "please call me Faye" Marin was conducted on a professional, clenched-smile basis, at least on my part.

Resplendent in a form-fitting, serpentine green dress, she sat front row center in what Ben dubbed the popcorn gallery. She offered her advice that if there were difficulties, she would consult the Spirit Masters.

"They're available to you and so is Amy's Higher Self." She frowned at me. "Carla, don't look at me that way. You were always so difficult. Your Higher Self is there for you. Whether you believe in it doesn't matter."

Her assistant, a young woman with spiky hair, brought her a Sprite and eyed me suspiciously.

Mike paid no attention to us as he set up recording equipment in a corner. True to form, he found his busy work for surviving the tension of the occasion.

"What Amy needs right now is to be connected to the Earth Mother below so she can be firmly grounded and to the universe above so she can feel a connection to the Spirit Masters," Faye said. "She desperately needs healing, Carla, desperately."

"I take it, Faye, you don't believe Amy is a disembodied spirit."

"She's obviously still in her body, temporally speaking, but in a state of complete dissociation." The first scientific word out of her mouth. "It happens more than you'd think."

"In an emotional sense, yes. We do have to feel to heal."

Make small talk, I told myself, trying to ignore Mike's pinched expression.

"I like that, Carla."

She had a throaty laugh that reminded me of Susan Sarandon. Her assistant appeared ready to kill on demand.

"I know you've got a full plate, sweetie," she told me. "But one more thing. It's important to allow the Higher Self to do its work. Isao feels a strong connection to Amy. That's the reason why he entered her while she was in a trance state, which means he may resist leaving. Your best hope at getting him to go is to enlist their Higher Selves."

By her own logic, her suggestion made no sense. If, by her explanation, she considered Isao to be a spectral visitor, why wouldn't he be completely Higher

Self? He had no body from which to be dissociated.

Rising from his seat, Rabbi Fleischer gave me a warm hug as another pair of arms folded around my waist. Nina. She wished me luck.

"I bet Amy's going to have one hell of a story about all this."

Her bravado was starting to fray around the edges.

I turned to the doorway to see a shaken Gordon and Randall, who was keeping his father upright. Rashida helped Randall guide Gordon to a seat, but before he made it all the way down, Gordon gave me a naked, fearful look.

"Get her back for me, please."

"I promise."

That was the wrong thing for me to say. Always be optimistic; never be specific. Yet, I could find no other way to handle the emotion of the moment, not with Dr. Nyanga and other Borlauch bigwigs watching us.

I entered the arena at almost the same time as Isao.

Amy had a long, disciplined runner's stride that, even when walking, gave the impression she was nearing a finish line. Isao moved with a dancer's grace, hardly seeming to brush the ground.

He took pride in the fact that, due to his skill at compensation, none of his directors or fellow actors ever knew about his bad knee. It had to have seemed a marvelous stroke of luck to find himself in such a sound, undamaged body. Not that he'd been able to go dancing, locked up in a psych ward.

Toni had arranged for covers from Amy's house to drape the bed, while the Durans brought a couple of potted plants from her study. They provided homey details to ease her return.

A single overhead light haloed us, leaving the watchers in shadows.

We were asking Isao to die again, an impression confirmed when Jiro walked over from talking to him.

"He feels very ashamed that, because he was upset about his wife, he got drunk and caused the truck to hit him," Jiro told us.

In one sentence, Jiro gave me more details about Isao's death than Isao granted in weeks of sessions.

"Now he has the chance to leave with dignity. He's grateful for his second chance."

Locating the microphone stand by the bed, Jiro went over to it as Isao began speaking.

"Isao wants to thank Ben for being a friend. He also wants to thank Dr. Akugawa for helping him when he first came here. Mister... Durans? The Duran family, he wants to apologize to you. He wants Amy to come back as much as you, and now you'll have your wish."

I heard Isao's mangling of my name. "Dr. Turner, he wants to thank you for caring about him. He's glad he got to know you."

Isao's face bore a hopeful expression tinged with dread.

So this was what it felt like, being the attending physician at an execution. No other way, I told myself.

I administered the injection and stepped back into the perimeter of the glow.

Jiro stood by the bed. He refused the chair Toni found for him.

I spoke into the microphone, hearing Toni turn down the nature sounds track a notch as I began. She came over and stood behind me. She would serve as my translator in case Jiro faltered.

I began the familiar cadence of relaxation, of letting go, but this time we would return to the street in Tokyo where he died. Jiro's voice softly provided the translation a beat behind.

T E N

She had been sleeping forever, dreaming a movie about the life of a Japanese man, starting in early childhood. At first, she felt stymied by the lack of subtitles. The words gradually began to make sense until she could follow the plot quite well.

The pacing, however, suffered from a documentary's devotion to realism. She hated the fact that the filmmakers had shot the entire documentary from the viewpoint of the hero, which meant she only saw his face in mirrors or reflected from ponds and shiny surfaces.

Through his eyes, she witnessed a big event in Isao's life. He seemed to be around five or six when his parents took him to a religious place where many other children stood dressed in their best clothes, waiting for the priest to come out.

Once the clip had run a few times, she understood that they were at a shrine and that the parents had brought the boy, his round-faced younger sister huddled next to him, to the shrine to seek the gods' protection. A robed priest entered the sanctuary, which acted as a trigger to the rest of the ritual. The children took turns ringing a giant bell, clapping hands to make the gods aware of their presence. The children said a prayer.

Although both siblings clutched bags of thousand year-old candy, the boy couldn't resist trying to take his sister's candy away until she burst into tears and fled for the comfort of their mother's arms. A cold dampness bit through his kimono. This told her that the time was late fall, but what year?

Amy enjoyed the time spent with Kaoru playing spin tops, hide-and-seek, and especially *janken-po.* Kaoru never grew bored with that game, pleading to play even when Isao made fun of her for crying when his rock broke her scissors too many times. That made it especially hard for Amy to watch when Isao grew older and stopped playing with his sister. He preferred the company of boys from school.

His older brother, Koichii, was a shy, delicate loner always buried in his books. That was a fate unlikely to happen to Isao, who loved music and art lessons more than any other school activity.

In other dreams she experienced, especially recurring ones, she could guide them to some degree in order to avoid nightmares. Yet she couldn't make Isao enjoy reading or rewrite that awful moment in the garden when the boy, sent home early for misbehavior, found the father of a schoolmate kissing his mother.

The odor of chrysanthemums hung heavy in the air. Isao walked by them and into the house, going directly to the room he shared with Koichii. A large *shoji* screen separated them from Kaoru's room. The scene always ended the same: Isao sat on a cushion painting with but a few strokes a portrait of his pet bell cricket, Ko, all the while ignoring his mother's efforts to explain away what happened.

His mother, pale and lovely, fell apart before Isao's eyes. Reduced to weeping for his forgiveness. Neither of them seemed to realize the peculiarity of a nine-year-old boy having this power over a woman.

Such a melodious sound came from the cricket all the while, a soprano "ri-i-in" stopped in mid-note when Isao reached into the cage and crushed Ko—his revenge on the mother who gave him the pet. Even so, Isao cried gut-wrenching tears over what he had done.

These were painful moments that, when replayed, never lost their poignancy, although Amy felt she understood the family better each time.

Isao adored his father. When Dr. Watanabe came home with gifts from his patients, he would ask Isao to carry them to an elderly widow who lived across the street.

His father seemed not to care whether the folded *furoshiki* cloth contained a colorful *obi,* a set of lacquer trays, a package of restorative dried plums, an amber bottle of American *sukotchi,* or toys. The contents went to the widow who always refused the gift at first.

After Isao insisted, as per his father's instructions, she would beckon the boy inside the entrance room, open up the cloth and praise the gift in extravagant terms, not letting him go until he'd eaten a mochi cake or downed a fruit drink.

Why his father wouldn't want to keep a box of candy mystified Isao, but to turn down toys? Finally, he went to his father, who was quietly reading under a paper lamp in his study, and asked the reason. Amy loved the soft lighting of Isao's house, so unlike the Western harshness of her childhood memories. It lent a warm radiance to even the hardest of moments for the boy.

Father put his book down on his black lacquered desk and asked with his customary mildness, "If your friend wanted one of your toys, would you give it to him?"

"Maybe, if I didn't want it too badly," Isao said honestly. "I'd let him have it."

"Mrs. Yoritomo would like to give presents to her grandchildren, but fortune hasn't smiled upon her. She's been kind to your mother and me."

With that, and without so much as a ruffle of the boy's hair—she didn't care for the comparative lack of physical intimacy in Japanese households—his father returned to his reading.

Isao thought over what his father had said, accepted it, and went on. Thus was virtue taught, by example rather than lecture.

One day Isao went to the widow's door with another gift. He found the door partly open and entered to find her dead in the kitchen. She had been stricken while preparing a dinner of rice and marinated eel. A doctor's son, Isao instinctively understood that he could do nothing more, so he ran to tell his parents.

That was but one moment in Isao's life, remembered in detail. However, the sparest of strokes daubed his war years.

Through jolting, horrific glimpses of battle—limbs soaring over Isao's head, screams of agony counterpointed by artillery barrages, his stumbling through a swamp of blood and excrement, an omnipresent feeling of fear—she learned more than she could ever have wanted to know about real warfare.

Absent throughout were any scenes of Isao shooting a gun or doing anything else of a violent nature.

"Time to wake up."

Was that Dr. Turner's voice coming from the window?

"Amy, it's time for you to open your eyes, feeling quite refreshed from your nap." Dr. Turner again.

She had been dreaming all along? Yet, so long a dream, and endlessly vivid.

From above, she saw a man sprawled on the street below. There were bystanders screaming for help, and huge neon signs flashing inane messages about whiskey and cigarettes. The crowd, the truck and the cars all vanished, leaving only the man, still lying face down, swathed in a cobalt glow. Underneath it all, Amy heard a static-ridden drone.

Suddenly, she stood on the street, staring down at Isao. No longer a grief-stricken child, he was now a grown man with the right side of his face crumpled and bloodied. Why had she been summoned to witness his life and death?

A curious synesthesia merged the glow and buzzing into one sensation, becoming louder and brighter by the moment, until a tendril of light and sound whisked out of Isao's body.

Impulsively, she thrust her hand into the stream and saw it dissolve. A burst of heat coursed through her body, as if she were in a direct conduit from one place to another. She saw people in the distance, their faces and forms indistinct. They were journeyers, she realized, from earlier times on this continuous pulse.

She would be next.

Waves, particles, whatever coursed through her at that moment had a coherent, laser-like quality yet seemed everywhere at once.

The street vanished into the gray void that surrounded her, the only relief being a faint golden glimmering somewhere to the... east? No, it felt like the west. Isao stood beside her, unhurt and smiling.

"Time for me to go, Amy."

He was already beginning to move toward the journeyers.

Such a generous, talented, graceful, and lovesick man. She appreciated his wit and bemoaned his inability to recognize when people took advantage of him.

"Don't leave, Isao."

"But it's your turn," he said.

She had only to wade into the stream and he would be gone, a lightning package of discrete memories, layered onto the ones who came before, wave upon wave without apparent end.

Impulsively, she latched onto his hand. "Come with me."

Not a step, but a singular kind of movement. She heard Isao gasp with surprise.

In one moment, they were there in gray obscurity. The next moment, in the now.

Light and sound erased the boundaries between the two, massing them into aural incandescence, free of time, free of space.

She opened her eyes.

Blinking until the room came into focus, she saw Dr. Turner standing next to the bed wearing a face made rigid by tension. A thirtyish Japanese man, much calmer, stood on the other side.

Isao tried to explain it to her. Something about the first session going wrong which forced them to go back in order to correct the problem.

"You should have let me go," he said. "They don't want me here. They're asking for you."

The voice inside her, the ghost in the machine. How could he be her in essence but so different, so much the Other?

Isao conjured an image of a rice paddy, the two of them on separate ends. Green shoots poked through the water. He walked toward her, his pants rolled up to mid-calf.

"Do you see? It's the same field, but you have your patch, and I have mine."

"So, how do we make the, uh, the same crop?"

A beautiful, sunlit day. Wasn't Isao a city boy? As if on cue, she experienced his memory of a teenage summer spent working on his uncle's farm.

Images struck her in oblique angles. A pretty neighbor girl kissing him during a festival in town, excited voices on the radio shouting that the eight corners of the world must be united by Japan under one roof, his cousin standing proudly in his naval uniform, paper boats in a stream. Lacerating visions stripped of their earlier dreamlike quality.

She told him to sleep, sleep as she had, give her time to adjust, learn her life the way she had his. Sleep, Isao. Dream. Lie down on your futon and sleep, please. I can't take this.

Gradually, the flood slowed to a trickle.

Images of a beloved actor on stage, Isao's mother standing on a railroad platform wearing a white apron and sash, waving goodbye as Isao went off to war, his father seated opposite him at a restaurant, looking wrinkled and small, so proud to meet Isao's intended.

Dream, Isao. Dream my dreams, she told him. Somehow, she'd figure out what to do. The other world within her stilled, and she fell back onto the bed, exhausted from the effort.

HAVING TALKED ISAO TO THE END OF HIS LIFE, HAVING ASKED WITHOUT HESITATION for him to die, I asked him to tell me what he saw.

Nothing, except a yellow light.

Walk toward it, I said, curious to know what he saw, but common sense took over midway. It was time to segue. Otherwise, he might recycle the same scenario.

Through Jiro, I told Isao to let go, to release himself from his surroundings. I saw his body go limp and at that moment, I called for Amy to wake up. I repeated it several times, making every effort to sound calm yet commanding.

Belle and I attended a healing service at a church toward the end of her life. We had tried every other physical and spiritual method available to us. Though a healing of Belle's emotions did take place, giving her the courage to face her last weeks, I felt cheated by the events of that night.

My wife had always been a believer. I approached faith in half-measures and equivocations, even more so now. I remained healthy and alive. And alone.

Rising halfway off the table, Amy stiffened, then her head fell back and her face took on an ecstatic glow, exactly like a believer in the spirit.

Did God choose her, through my actions, for this? Had God found all of us, save Amy, lacking? Or had it been nothing more than blind, atheistic luck?

Almost shouting her name, I watched as she slumped back to the table and finally, blessedly, lifted her head.

Amy's eyes stared back at me.

ELEVEN

He whom God has touched will always be a being apart; he is, whatever he may do, a stranger among men; he is marked by a sign.
—Ernest Renan

AMY'S BROTHER AND NEPHEW CAME DOWNSTAIRS FROM THE OBSERVATION ROOM, rapidly followed by Nina. Amy gazed exhaustedly at Rabbi Fleischer, who had finished leading a prayer of thanks.

Every light in the building seemed to be at maximum luminescence. I squinted at Toni Akugawa and pointed out the obvious, that it would be a while before we could do a thorough examination.

Toni glanced up at the gallery. "We need to leave while the gettin's good and have Amy and her family meet us over at her house. We'll check her out there. Gordon's made it clear she's not staying under this roof one second longer than necessary."

The charge nurse brought me Amy's chart so I could write discharge orders while Ben raced upstairs to pick up Amy's gear. He looked uncomfortable around her. It had to be hard on him, losing a friend that no one else seemed to miss at all.

Giving his sister another hug, Gordon took off for the hospital's business office with a Borlauch rep in tow while I gathered my equipment.

A short time later, Amy smiled at me calmly and left with her family.

Rashida appeared at my side. "I wish you had talked to Uncle Mike before he left. I think that Nigerian bitch fired him."

"That's not polite. Borlauch has just dodged a major lawsuit. There's still a chance Ms. Duran might sue them."

On the way to Amy's house, we picked up a couple of pizzas I ordered by phone. No one needed to cook on a day like this. Odysseus, Seeley's Sister, and the Prodigal Child had finally come home. Time to celebrate.

I was not the only one to think ahead. Randall had already laid out a supply of chips, dips, and beer, while others must have also made stops because there were several containers of salads, empanadas, organic sweets, and bottles of wine.

Amy entered the kitchen and poured a glass of water. She was dressed in khaki shorts and a Longhorn tee shirt.

"Are you hungry?" Rabbi Fleischer asked.

"Starving. I haven't eaten in almost three weeks." True enough.

Gordon arrived about the time Amy started in on a slice of carrot cake. Randall had thoroughly dissected the last of the NBA playoffs, including the earlier elimination of her beloved Rockets.

"I can't believe I missed that. Gordon, what else happened? Did we declare war on anyone new?"

"Nope, not even Borlauch."

"Punks."

That came from both Rashida and Randall, who seemed well on their way to becoming friends.

Amy seemed back to normal. She cracked a mild joke about Randall's ginger beer—"don't let the name fool you"—well contained until Nina brought the party to a crashing halt.

"What did you see?"

Toni caught my eye with a gesture toward the hallway. "If you don't mind, we're going to visit with Amy for a little bit."

"Um, we can use my study." Amy leapt to her feet and led the way. She left the question unanswered until we had settled into our chairs.

"Dr. Turner, Dr. Akugawa." Amy sat back in her chair and cocked her head to one side. "You're not going to believe what happened."

Although we tried not to interrupt her narrative, it proved impossible. A sound and light conduit of pure energy, connecting her to, presumably, her past lives?

Somber-faced, Amy told us that she witnessed nothing of a conventionally spiritual nature during the second session.

"All I saw was a light on the horizon that might have been anything. Maybe it led to the world to come. I don't know. The strangest part to me is that I never once questioned the reality of what was happening."

Toni shook her head. "There's a gap of several years between his death and your birth. Even if there's something to your story, you can't explain that away."

"Is there a rule that the transition has to happen immediately? Maybe I needed a break, or maybe I skipped a life during the first session. Maybe time is experienced differently there. I don't know. I'm just the one who went through it, that's all."

I could tell the two could go at that topic for a while, so I stepped in. I asked Amy to talk about Isao, whom she had barely mentioned to this point. She stumbled over her words as she described the boy she followed to school, the man she watched fall apart over a spiteful woman, the Isao she came to know so intimately.

"I couldn't let him go like that."

Toni made no effort to veil her skepticism.

"It sounds as though you formed an intense emotional attachment to Isao, who is, according to you—"

"My former life." She said it with a bemused expression. "It's not a romantic thing, Dr. Akugawa. He died for nothing, for a nobody, yet he cared so much."

"You wanted to fix the situation." I realized what she was trying to tell us. "So you asked him to come along."

"More or less."

Toni glared at us, plainly frustrated. "He's still in there. Is that what you're saying?"

"I'm sorry, but yes."

"Oh, God."

Toni went over to the window and inspected a nearby willow tree, trying to regain her composure.

"He's sleeping right now," Amy said with a helpful air. "Um, I can't handle him. Not yet anyway. I asked him to dream my dreams for a while and get to know me the same way I came to know him."

Without preamble, Toni spun around and delivered a stream of Japanese.

Amy looked pained. "I'm sorry. Whenever I talk Japanese or try to think in it, it stirs up Isao and things get complicated."

"I don't see how the situation is tenable," I told her. "You can't possibly balance two separate identities, whatever you decide to label them."

Amy's voice was soft but firm.

"I have two sets of memories, but I'm one person. It's as if I've had amnesia all this time and couldn't remember Isao. Now I do, and right now, he's learning my memories. We have to work this out. We need to come up with a solution that doesn't involve killing him again. I won't stand for it."

After that, a more conventional examination took place. When completed, it convinced us that our patient experienced no lingering aftereffects from her time away, unless one counted her belief that she was hosting her past life.

Amy, who seemed grateful to be done with the interrogation, returned to her party while Toni and I decided upon a course of action.

Further hospitalization was out of the question for the time being. Not only would Gordon refuse to sign the papers, Amy's well-oriented demeanor would prevent any judge from agreeing to a forced committal.

"Do you really believe Isao is her past life?" Toni dialed her volume down a few notches. "All we've done with this session is validate Isao, and now she's not about to let go of him. If Borlauch couldn't come up with a smoking gun, then there is no gun, period. But what if Isao had been in purgatory all this time then moved in while Amy was out of the building?

"I know how stupid it sounds, but I'm telling you, there are a number of theories that explain what happened, theories that aren't predicated on her reeling in her past life. Past is past, Carla."

I, too, had been wrestling with the meaning of Isao's now-continuing visit.

When Jesus Christ died, the Holy Spirit supposedly became manifest. While the Holy Spirit is a full-fledged member of the Trinity, no one has claimed that the Holy Spirit downloaded God the Father and God the Son into its matrix.

For Toni, a practicing Catholic, this case posed a serious challenge to her beliefs. For me, faith had been lacking for quite some time. I didn't know what to make of what had happened. I only knew that Amy had returned.

DR. AKUGAWA MADE AN ABRUPT EXIT THROUGH THE FRONT DOOR, NOT BOTHERING to say goodbye.

"What was that all about?" Nina asked, mildly concerned, but she was more interested in listening to Amy's description of Isao's visits to Tokyo clubs in the 1950s. He had seen Oscar Peterson, Ella Fitzgerald, and other jazz greats. They played in smoke-filled venues packed with young people who had worn out their treasured albums.

"Can you sing like a bird?" Gordon asked with a huge smile.

"Don't even ask."

If she sang, would Isao take over? It would be hard for him not to, listening to her butcher a tune. This grand gesture, this invitation of hers, threatened to go off the rails at any moment.

When Dr. Akugawa asked her in Japanese what she was trying to achieve, Amy couldn't come up with any more to say than that she didn't have any agenda in mind. Isao stirred from slumber to ask if something was wrong. He even projected an image of himself with his hair mussed and eyes sleep-filled.

It brought to mind an old Jorge Amado novel, *Dona Flor and Her Two Husbands,* in which Flor, and only Flor, could see her first husband, a good-timing lothario who died during Carnival.

A dead man haunted Amy, taking up residence inside her skull. Rabbi Fleischer knew something was wrong. While he nibbled on a curried cauliflower empanada, he kept his eyes on Amy in a familiar loving, but measuring, mode.

Regardless of what anyone thought, she knew Isao wasn't a ghost. She had felt the conduit swallow her hand in a river of painless fire, seen the lives behind her, and the yawning gap ahead. Next in line, she simply asked the last occupant to stay on. Maybe it wasn't that tidy a resolution, not with a house full of company thinking Isao had left.

How could she and Isao maintain their boundaries over time?

Their arrangement was bound to disintegrate, which would land her where precisely? Mixed up with Isao and vice-versa? How strange that a person who hated any loss of control set herself up for the ultimate invasion of personal space. A poetic sort of justice.

She could feel Isao inside her, working hard to be unobtrusive, trying to sleep. She had had the advantage of beta-anodynol and Carla's hypnosis to keep her out of his way. She couldn't wake up, or could she have if she had tried?

Maybe what happened was that she expected to relax, to do nothing, and so she never rose out of Isao's dreams. In the meantime, what did she gain by keeping her family and friends from knowing the truth, especially if it all fell apart one day at work or at any moment, for that matter?

She took a deep breath and tried to steady her voice before beginning. "Um, guys?"

Randall stopped in the middle of an anecdote.

"There's something I need to tell you."

TWELVE

WHAT A STRANGE LITTLE GIRL.

She cleaned an already pristine bedroom until it looked to Isao like something one would see in a magazine spread—"this is what forward-thinking Americans are doing to modernize their homes"—then she would go outside to shoot baskets alone in their driveway until late in the evening.

Ben had told him that in America girls played team sports. There weren't any girls with her in the driveway.

Even several years after the suicide, she still returned to images of her father arguing with her mother. He was a sad, distant man uncomfortably lodged in her past, troubling in a way that puzzled Isao. Had Father been so unusual? It did seem to him that other fathers were such gruff, overblown creatures.

She seemed to remember almost nothing from the time of her father's suicide. How fortunate that Masao had missed out on his father's death, which Isao understood now to be the result of a drunk gone disastrously wrong and not an intentional act.

Watching the young Amy made him miss his sister all the more. Such a tender-hearted, gentle girl. How could he have fallen in line with his friends so easily, dumping her like that? Kaoru had been in his thoughts so often during those awful days in the Philippines. Best not to think of that time, he reminded himself.

Images of Kaoru came into his mind unbidden: the devoted sister who waited at the train station when he came home from the war, the girl who had grown into a hollow-eyed woman with a sickly cough.

Since his months in a Dutch POW camp had put some much-needed flesh on his bones, he was appalled to see the war's effect on her. Mother died earlier during a firebombing attack, removing a mouth to feed, but that left Kaoru struggling to keep the household going, the two servants and their families fed while Father was away.

Father had been drafted into medical service in Manchuko, a fate shared by Isao's brother, an intern.

He fumbled through his bag and found a package of American chocolate. She devoured the bar, even licked the wrapping at the end, all the while apologizing between swallows for her rudeness.

Their bus ride home took them through neighborhoods alternately charred and booming, gutters clotted with human waste, until they came to a chaotic street where they got off and walked the rest of the way. They dodged bicycles and the occasional Allied Jeep filled with huge, cheerful soldiers who tossed candy to children scrabbling fiercely on stick legs.

The house looked scorched and desolate, much the worse for wear. Kaoru and the servants had moved most of the household furnishings into the storehouse out back. Its thick earthen walls and tiled roof provided ample protection for their possessions as well as themselves during wartime air raids.

Most of their possessions ended up being sold for food and fuel, but at least they had something to bargain with. Too many skeletal figures wandered the street who had been stripped of all possessions, and in some cases, of their sanity. Silent, gaunt, maimed veterans. Kaoru, his loving sister, was just as ghostly. She died several months later of tuberculosis and the aftereffects of malnourishment.

Father and Koichii's return, better food distribution by the Americans, Isao's money-raising efforts like arranging dates for GIs, one of his less shady enterprises. All of it came too late for Kaoru.

That was one reason why he had such trouble with Amy's weight mania.

He pushed ahead to her teenage years, curious to know more about that period in American lives. While she seemed to get out more, going on dates with boys and playing basketball games, her fixation on weight became worse, supplemented by occasional bouts of vomiting. Then it seemed as though she would find ways to undermine her peculiar devotion.

She ate high-calorie shakes, ice cream, or candy right before bedtime. Hard for her to stick a finger down her throat while asleep. He found it so frustrating, given the immense wealth of her country, that she would reject meals that Kaoru would have walked across half of Tokyo to... not eat. Kaoru would have eaten very little, reserving the rest in a *furoshiki* to take home.

Amy's pristine dates with boys became physical encounters with girls. Isao recalled an actress in Tokyo rumored to have dated Marlene Dietrich. Such an exotic creature, he thought at the time. Amy's dates, while attractive enough, lacked Dietrich's combustible charm. How disappointing.

Without making any effort, he picked up quite a bit of English during Amy's dreams. The knowledge somehow sank into him at a deep level, the way the melody to a jazz tune used to pop out of him note-perfect despite the fact he hadn't spent a moment learning it.

Amy didn't listen to jazz, but during her college years, he listened along with her at concerts and clubs, developing along the way a taste for funk and other African-American sounds.

However, he couldn't get country. Some of the women sang well, but the melodies were so simple as to verge on primitive. If I'm staying with her, he thought, we're going to buy some jazz records. Classical music, he could take that in small measures, and her violin practice less than that. She played well enough, but with no apparent passion.

And it wouldn't have hurt her to attend more plays instead of only the occasional musical. Some of them were highly entertaining, like the one on the riverboat, but why no Shakespeare? The great Shakespeare, that most brilliant visionary, had to be seen live.

He adored Kubota's production of *Hamlet*, set in medieval Edo. He attended every performance and ended up volunteering to work under the prop master.

Why would Amy, so fond of literature, be deaf to her people's most noble representative?

The present reached out to him, despite his having buried himself as deeply as possible in her memories. How peculiar, to look at the world through the eyes of a tall American woman. She owned perfect vision and a right knee that never gave her a moment's worry.

It surprised him how little her being a woman bothered him, even when he had been inside her all alone. After that first night, he found himself stuck in a hospital with no female lover around and no female complaints to confuse his responses. He struck up male friendships and behaved as a man with no one forcing him to do otherwise.

What of his present situation?

He hadn't been a good Buddhist, but he absorbed enough of it to know that death follows life in a natural progression, its cycle of suffering nothing to get upset about, while he had examined his vague ideas about reincarnation even less.

Now he was stuck inside a gaijin body in twenty-first century America. He had a reputation for being individualistic. But seeing how that attitude worked in the future present, he had only been unusual in Japanese terms.

Thoughts about the next millennium had rarely crossed his mind since it was too far in the future to be worth considering. Yet he found himself in a science-fiction world, complete with tiny phones, computers that weren't the size of a pachinko parlor, and many other marvels.

In his day, everyone knew Americans would get to the moon, although he was disappointed to learn they did nothing after that. Japan would have set up a base and made it a going operation. Why go to all the trouble of going there in the first place?

Americans were impractical yet dynamic, great dreamers but not much on the long view. The proof? Amy's doctor and the drug company researcher hadn't bothered to consider what would happen if they succeeded.

It spoke well for Dr. Turner that she admitted to Amy she had acted rashly. The Borlauch people had yet to apologize.

He glided forward in her memories. Amy's lover, the power-mad realtor. Why had Amy tolerated her lover for so long and stayed in a job she hated? She didn't live in Japan, where it took courage to quit a lifetime *salariman* position in order to become an actor. A stupid kind of courage, he had to admit.

Finally, she left the realtor and quit the job that both created so much heartache. Dr. Turner, an elegant, scholarly woman entered the scene, blessed with a spotlight any lead actor would find blinding. This intensity of attraction made Amy willing to explore her feelings about her father's suicide. How strange that the event itself remained swathed in fog.

Restless, he felt so restless now. So many more memories to plumb if he wanted, but he understood the outline, grasped the gist of the language.

There, over the barrier she constructed, he could see the world through her eyes in a jumble of impressions not always adding up to a coherent view. Amy had so many books at her job. Many recorded on shiny plates, while the paper books came in a staggering array of colors and shapes.

The people were just as varied. He had thought of Americans as being mostly tall Europeans. However, the variety of Caucasians who roamed through Amy's store matched the variety of books.

Africans came through in many shades and appearances, few of them resembling the jazz musicians and soldiers who visited Tokyo. He saw Asians of all kinds and shoppers who resembled tame versions of Hollywood Mexican bandits. It was a shame that the Indian women rarely dressed in saris. Their beauty had only added to the pleasure of watching Sajiyat Ray's movies.

He considered himself to be enlightened about social prejudices. Why disdain *burakumin* for being outsiders, or suspect Koreans living in Japan of being disloyal? Here, he saw that philosophy carried out to its logical conclusion and wondered how people kept their bearings.

He knew going-along with the status quo caused the deaths of so many of his classmates, but there was something to knowing one's place in the general scheme of things.

What was he thinking? He hated his company job and couldn't wait to get out once he earned enough acting jobs to make it possible. No, the American way might be scarier and prone to mistakes, but far more flexible.

AMY'S FIRST DAY BACK AT BOOKISH FELT AWKWARD FROM THE MOMENT HER BOSS entered her cubicle to say he had complete confidence in her mental stability. He watched her from the periphery several times that day as she handled customer complaints, did the setup for their visiting author, and tackled an enormous backlog of work.

Her favorite barista volunteered to make her a cup of green tea. "I heard you're into Japanese stuff. I know how to do it the traditional way."

"I'd rather have my usual cappuccino."

She kept herself from pointing out that Isao practically lived in coffeehouses back in the 1950s.

The rest of the week went much better at work, although her concentration still felt broken into shards by the effort of ignoring Isao.

A magenta-haired sales assistant brought her a little Buddha, saying Amy could put it in her pocket for good luck. Thanking her for the gift, Amy couldn't resist asking the girl what she had heard.

"That you had a bad drug reaction. The doctor and that investigator asked a lot of questions about Japan. Somebody said they thought you'd been raised there. Is that what happened?"

"No, I didn't revert to my childhood."

Farther back than that, actually. Amy asked her who'd given her the information. An investigator, the girl said. That didn't surprise Amy, although she did think Randall was probably wrong about company operatives shadowing Amy. That sounded too much like a spy novel. What did Borlauch care what happened to her going forward? She promised not to sue them; they promised to pay her hospital bills. Story over, as far as they knew.

Amy met Nina for lunch at a nearby cafe where she ate an eggplant sandwich with a lemon soda. Nina, for one, had no problem accepting that Isao was camping out in her best friend's brain. Nina's only question was whether Amy and Isao were going to take turns being in control, or were they going to cut a deal, as she put it.

Dr. Turner wanted another session, one in which Isao would be asked firmly to step aside, but she wanted to keep using the experimental drug. No, thanks. Dr.

Akugawa had suggested an alternative session. Who knew what that was about?

Dr. Jiro Endo, a Borlauch researcher present at the session, kept leaving messages that she should call him. Those requests needed to stay unfulfilled if she wanted to avoid speaking, worse yet, thinking in Japanese.

All the while, Isao grew stronger. His medusa presence prowled at the perimeter, exuding traces of his memories, his ideas, his reactions, giving every indication that he wanted to stay in her world.

Our world, she said to herself, half believing it, half wishing she never walked into that office, blithely thinking she could do Dr. Turner a favor in return for beta-anodynol's erasure of her eating disorder.

Nina thought it amazing Amy could work given such distractions, but during much of her life, anorexia provided its own constant soundtrack, souring moments that should have been victories. Was it worth getting rid of that only to gain another companion, one far more invasive? Had she even slept the last three nights?

While it helped to talk to Rabbi Fleischer, she couldn't keep cutting into his sleep. He declined to pass judgment about Isao, seeming to accept his reality, if not Amy's belief about his origin.

She always struggled with the life-after-death question. At some point, she chose to shut down Ms. Raging Intellect and simply trust that it would all make sense someday. That would have continued to be a workable strategy had she stayed home one Thursday evening. While dining out with Nina one day, Amy thought of how she didn't know what to believe anymore. Her personal theology required a place for Isao, even as she struggled to keep him under control.

"Amy?" She had the feeling Nina must have said her name several times.

"Sorry. You were saying?"

Nina, who looked even more incandescent than usual, was dressed in a sheer plum blouse and gold lamé wraparound skirt. She compared Amy's situation to *All of Me*, an old movie with Steve Martin and Lily Tomlin.

Amy thought it amusing how Martin and Tomlin controlled different halves of their body. That hadn't happened yet with her and Isao—thank God. Nothing, as far as she knew, remotely came close to her experience.

Absent-mindedly, she whisked crumbs off the table into her hand, then dumped them into a napkin, folded it and tucked a corner under her plate.

"No, think of it, Duran. Tomlin jumped into the body of this flaming hot con artist and the con artist went into a beautiful white horse."

"Happy ending. I remember. Martin and Tomlin dancing up a storm. That won't work, Nina. For one thing, I can't dance."

"I've seen your footwork. No news flash there. I'm not saying to shove Isao into a horse's body. I've thought about it. But horses aren't the most intelligent of animals, which means Isao would be in there for years waiting for Black Beauty to kick off."

"Nina—"

"You know, being able to race in the Kentucky Derby. Wouldn't that be a killer."

Amy studied her friend's face. As sincere as a Sunday morning choir girl. Which could only mean one thing.

"I hate it when you pull my leg."

They both dissolved into laughter, causing the Rastafarian couple at the next table to frown at them.

When Nina came up for air, she said, "I know it's an impossible situation. I can't imagine what I'd do."

"Try."

Her face looked fearful. "I'd let him in, but that's not a solution, really. That's just, what else can you do?" Nina looked over Amy's shoulder. "Crap."

Amy turned and saw Dr. Akugawa approaching their table, accompanied by a woman who looked familiar. Dr. Faye Marin, the celebrity psychologist Nina said had been at the hospital session and the same Faye Marin who had been leaving phone messages for weeks. One more reason why Amy rarely checked her cell phone anymore.

Marin wore a relaxed expression, counterpointed by Akugawa's gloom.

"I hope you don't mind me dropping in," Marin said. "Since I'm in town for a seminar, I decided to check in with you. Your coworkers told me where to find you."

And none of them thought to warn her. Why wouldn't she welcome a visit from a celebrity? Hardly.

Amy chose diplomacy. "I appreciate your coming by to see me." Now, the push-back. "However, I don't wish to participate in any more studies."

"That's right," Nina said. "Y'all can forget about giving her that drug."

Dr. Akugawa had a similar edge to her voice. "This isn't about the beta-anodynol. I'm most certainly not in league with Borlauch."

Marin sat down beside them uninvited, followed by a stiff-acting Dr. Akugawa.

After giving her drink order to the waiter, who'd suddenly become more attentive, Marin gave everyone her trademark enamel-bleached smile.

"I realize that this is a very difficult time for you and your visitor. But, it may be time for you to consider the truth of what's happening. You channeled his spirit during that first session. The reason he won't leave is because you share issues of suicide and abandonment."

"Isao didn't kill himself," Amy said with some annoyance. "He was so blind drunk he walked into the street without looking and got hit by a truck. When we went through it the second time, he understood what happened. Besides, take any two people. You're bound to find some similarities."

Both doctors looked at her strangely.

Dr. Akugawa spoke first. "Ms. Duran, it's not plausible that Isao's a past life or a spirit of some kind. My concern is for your emotional state. Isao is attempting another takeover, and you're doing nothing to stop him. You cannot unlive your past. Isao isn't your father. If you allow him to gain psychological dominance, you may never break free again."

"Isao is me, and I am him. You could say we're links in a chain. I have to find a way to get him to return to his link, to subside into his layer. He needs to understand that I can't handle his memories, his emotions. You don't have to believe me, but if you really want to do some good here, tell me how to tamp him down."

"This is what I'm proposing." Marin accepted her coffee without glancing at the waiter, whose adoring look went unnoticed. "We provide you with a private session in which your visitor is guided to a higher spiritual plane, however differently you and I define that plane of existence."

"Why would I want to work with you?"

"I'm writing my book, regardless of whether you participate. I have more than enough material from my sources."

Amy looked over at Dr. Akugawa, who had the grace to appear embarrassed.

Marin continued. "I'm committed to the seal of secrecy and would never dream of breaking it."

"You'd get your ass sued, that's why," Nina said.

Amy rolled her eyes.

"This is what *I* propose: the two of you come over to my house tomorrow night, eight o'clock sharp. I'll have a couple of my friends there. No cameras, no media. Please don't try to slip in any talk of Spirit Masters. I don't believe in them. What I need you to do is to explain the situation to Isao and leave. That should be sufficient."

When Amy got home, she went on a long, satisfying run, one that made her lungs burn and her calves clamp down until the endorphins kicked in for the last few blocks. It gave her a rush that made it hard to keep from tacking on some more distance, stretching her limits as much as she could. Afterward, as she cooled down while walking around on her lawn, she was glad she showed some restraint.

Gods, her legs hurt. It reminded her of the time her platoon went on a forced march during those weeks before they'd shipped out. To her, it seemed that they'd marched for the pure hell of it, just to see who would fall out from the heat. No one did, although Shikeda spent the night in the barracks groaning from the pain of his swollen and probably broken ankle.

She sat on the front porch steps, her water bottle toppled over onto a rosebush. Isao's memory, not hers. Why did the images seem so crisp, the emotions still so raw?

Too many tendrils reaching her now, messy images impossible to contain.

THIRTEEN

A BONE-TIRED MIKE SAGGED INTO MY LIVING ROOM SOFA WITH THE AIR OF A MAN who cared little what happened to him. Thankfully, Rashida was out with friends, as she would have been shocked to see him looking so bedraggled.

Stubble missed by his razor, an unwashed polo shirt, he hadn't looked this bad since—not even his divorce hit him this hard. Borlauch indeed fired him and hired him back the next day. Dr. Nyanga wanted to make a point. Point made, Dr. Nyanga asked him to devise a study of beta-anodynol's effectiveness in inducing states much like what occurred with Amy. An appalling thought.

"Mike, there's no way you can control the outcome."

"Yeah, the language problem. We've developed a master list of translators we can contact at a moment's notice, but we shouldn't have to go to them because IBM has an excellent language recognition program via a mainframe at Stanford. We establish a link with it and use voice-activated software already on the market so that we can understand the first words out of the past persona's mouth almost instantly. We identify the primary tongue, if necessary link to the human translator, and we have it covered both ways. If we set it up properly, the current life will be able to translate for the past. We just need the support system in place for purpose of documentation."

"There are and have been thousands of languages, not all of them well studied or possessing living translators," I reminded him.

"No offense, Carla, but we didn't know beans about what we were doing that night. We sent that poor woman off to meet her past life without bothering to prepare her for the shock. No wonder she went into a catatonic state. We're damned lucky she's so stable we were able to bring her back. One of your little parlor neurotics would still be spinning in the psych unit right now. Damned lucky."

His eyes drifted off to some other reference point.

"That's why you shouldn't be trying this with someone else. The odds against it working are phenomenal," I said.

Amy sounded so guarded over the phone the last time—when was it, Tuesday?—unwilling to come in for a session or even to talk about what she was going through. Nor were Gordon and Randall helpful, as they both believed Amy found a way to handle Isao's presence.

Gordon hadn't wanted to spend time on the phone discussing his sister's mental state.

"Look, Doctor," he'd said. "Last weekend, she trimmed hedges and edged her lawn before dragging me off to the synagogue with her. She seems kind of freaked about the situation, but she's handling it about as well as anyone could."

That was more than could be said about Mike who lit up a Winston without asking my permission. Old habits died hard.

"Carla, there's no way I'd put someone through such an experience, however controlled, without knowing with absolute certainty what the procedure entails. That's why I'm the first guinea pig—second, if you count Amy."

By the time Rashida came home hours later with a couple of espresso shakes, I had talked myself hoarse trying to shake Mike from his plan, unsurprised by my lack of success with a man who once ran five miles in a rainstorm just to see how it felt.

Why wouldn't he want to know what was behind the curtain? Why didn't I? Through his impassioned rhetoric, he caused me to think that it might be possible to visit with one's past life without it pitching a tent in one's present.

In the days after the second session or, as Mike now insisted on calling it, the "procedure," he e-mailed scanned photos and other documents, much of it with accompanying translations, all of it detailing Isao's life. Borlauch had previously declined to share these details with me or with Amy's family.

Isao's school transcript was hardly a bombshell. He had been an average student in most subjects, but exceptional in anything having to do with poetry and drama. He earned good marks in Mandarin, the one foreign language he appeared to have studied.

There were stills from several television appearances, posters of contemporary plays in which he usually had the largest supporting role, plus a strange cop drama in which he played the lead role of a Robin Hood gangster with Buddha-like qualities.

He was a man more pretty than handsome, who aged well but, having started late on an acting career, died before he could achieve the sort of fame that causes people to idolize Heath Ledger and Tupac Shakur.

On the way home from dropping Mike off at the airport, I called Imani. Dear Imani. She reported that she was ready to move to Tennessee anytime I wanted because "the air is like wet all the time, but most of the time we're in the gym and it's so great, I'm having a great time, learning all kinds of neat stuff, like a good post-up move—did Grandma tell you I've grown a quarter of a inch since I got here?—and it's so cool, you gotta come see me shake 'n bake, Mama, you just gotta."

Mama had to take a rain check, had to sound calm, had to give a lame excuse. Both Mike and Nyanga wanted an experienced professional at the helm in Chicago. Me. If I didn't accept, one of the psychiatrists present for the second session would do the job. Mike held out the carrot that the experience might teach us how to deactivate Isao, although I had my doubts. He resisted removal twice already.

They thought I could convince Amy to participate in yet another session. That was the real reason they made the offer. Before Borlauch could send Mike off on his harebrained expedition, the company wanted to prove that they could extract, examine, and safely return a past life.

Rashida had been uncommonly quiet during the last of the argument, preferring to sip on her shake and listen, wide-eyed about the prospect of Uncle Mike ending up like Amy.

Now, with him gone, she sat in my favorite recliner, a throw pillow clutched over her stomach. She looked as unsettled as I felt.

"Are you going to do it?"

"I don't know. It might be the only way to make Amy better. We don't have a clue how to undo the first mistake."

"So you're going to make a new mistake. Uncle Mike's upset with himself over what happened, and you know him, he always has to do something to fix a problem. He can't step back and let it heal itself."

The phone rang. It was Nina, who said she was calling from Amy's bathroom. Marin and Toni Akugawa had roped Amy into what sounded like a de-facto exorcism. Rabbi Fleischer had just arrived, but Gordon and Randall were out of town.

"She hasn't been sleeping. She's afraid to let go. She says she's having moogen. It sounds something like moogen even though she's not asleep. I'm thinking dreams. Or nightmares. Please hurry. I have a bad feeling about this."

F O U R T E E N

IT HAD BEEN AMY'S IDEA TO CONDUCT THE SESSION IN HER OWN HOME, WITH NO more past-life theater for medical gawkers, thank you very much.

The sound of cushions compressing nearby told her that Dr. Akugawa had settled in the recliner, while Dr. Marin was already sitting on an ottoman beside the sofa.

Before they ever set foot in her home, she established by phone the ground rules: no drugs of any kind, no references by Dr. Marin to goddesses or spirits, only to the singular God. Shut Isao up, but don't try to erase him. If Amy felt uncomfortable at any time, they had to leave. And to make sure they didn't take liberties, Rabbi Fleischer positioned himself nearby.

"Amy?" He was on his knees beside the sofa. "You don't have to go through with this."

"I know. Um, the thing is, I don't think he's a ghost. He's me, but if there's a way to keep him quiet, I'm all for it."

Dr. Turner should have tried listening, instead of harping on drug therapies and treatments. After the second session, she had to know nothing standard could work.

Okay. It was time to stretch out and let Dr. Marin start talking. Friends close, the pillow so inviting.

Jangling images from a dead man's life—cherry blossoms, the sensuous view of the nape of a woman's neck, a frightened soldier standing next to a tree—all of that and too much more thrust in and out of view. She could feel Isao holding back then rushing forward over and over, the waves pushing closer to her shore.

Marin began talking quietly to her about the heaviness in her arms. Amy, heaving a deep sigh of relief, stopped fighting Isao. She managed to send off a Hebrew prayer, the *Shema*, barely verbalized in her mind, before she lost touch with everything beyond her eyelids.

No barrier at all between the two sides now. In a frenzied cloud of sound and radiance, Isao's thoughts hurtled down a wide concourse farther and farther into her own individual unique mine mine mine Amy Luz Duran.

She could no longer see him in the shadows over their rice paddy. Between her feet the shoots rose higher and higher until she began running in waist-high lush grass toward the tangled undergrowth of a tropical jungle, chased by an emotion that caught up to her at the jungle's edge.

I am a strange beast. No longer human, now capable of monstrous acts. *Shikata ga nai.* It can't be helped. There is no other way. Shikata ga nai.

Suddenly, she stood face-to-face with a nut-brown man dressed in rags who swung a machete at her head. Ducking at the last moment, she discovered a rifle in her hand and used the butt end to knock him down. With a smooth motion, she bayoneted the man in the throat then left him there sprawled on the ground, his blood gushing in an oddly graceful fountain.

I can't waste bullets right now, she thought. It'll draw the enemy. I'll have a pack of crazed Filipino peasants chasing me right into the Americans. Shikata ga nai.

Another step and farther back in time. She was helping guard a platoon of American soldiers, captured during retreat from Mount Latib.

One of the gaijin, his jaw a mottled heap of bones and flies, kept up a monotonous cry. He lay under a tree that provided no relief from the suffocating heat. The other gaijins, unable to stop his noisemaking, watched apprehensively as she walked over. They were nothing but weaklings, but like them, she was being eaten alive by fungus and insects in this miserable excuse for a country.

Amy dispatched the gaijin with a bullet to the head, then went over to her tent and drank down a canteen of tepid water. Gods, what a horrible place. Shikata ga nai.

Fast forward. Panicked, she struggled to escape a tent rapidly going up in flames. Singed, she limped into the jungle on legs at turns numb and excruciating. She hadn't a clue which way to go. All points led to the Americans. At random, she began slicing a path through the brush with a machete torn from the hand of a dying man.

Corporal Suga came up beside her, babbling that they were the last survivors. They had no choice but to kill themselves before the Americans found them and cut off their testicles.

"We've got to do it, Watanabe. You can't walk any farther, and I'm all out of cartridges."

Suga had been a willing toady to Sgt. Yoritomo, always thrilled to fuck the sergeant's leftovers. He liked to steal food from the rest of the platoon and present it to Yoritomo as a gift. Suga was the stupidest soldier in the entire 16th Division, who managed to survive when far better men had died.

"Do you have any clean clothes?" she asked.

"No."

"How unfortunate."

Amy pulled out her pistol and shot him in the chest. She stumbled away, not bothering to watch him fall. Minutes later, she stopped hacking through the brush and fell backwards, exhausted. She saw a full moon slivered by branches. The moon gave her not one trace of enlightenment. Pulling out her pistol, she aimed it at her belly and pulled the trigger. Nothing happened. She'd used her last bullet on Suga.

Sunlight. Jumping back farther in time, she stood at the edge of the jungle, a rifle in her hands. She could hear behind her a woman's voice, crying feebly, as Suga and two others took turns mounting the whore, laughter ringing out over the sounds each made when taking their pleasure.

Amy hated being near the gaijin camps. She much preferred going on patrols where the enemy wasn't tucked meekly behind barbed wire, but others in the squad enjoyed the softer comforts of the kind of women found wherever soldiers gathered. This *joro* refused Corporal Suga's offer of a clutch of eggs and was now paying the price for her lack of cooperation.

"Watanabe, it's your turn now."

Taking Amy's rifle, Suga turned her around.

"Such a delicate boy," he said with a knowing smile. "Please do me the honor of accepting this most humble present."

It would be rude to turn him down, and insults from the older men would become unbearable if she didn't take her turn. Plastering a smile on her face, she unbuckled her belt and slowly unzipped her trousers. Shikata ga nai.

She jumped forward to just after killing Suga. Moonlight rippled overhead, a glow striated by wind-driven branches. Wind carried the sickly sweet stench of death strewn over miles of swampy terrain. She couldn't go on and she couldn't stay.

Amy murdered countless people, raped a helpless woman out of pure cowardice, and couldn't even manage to kill herself with the enemy closing in.

She was so lacking in honor, she erased over four years from her life because it failed to fit her self-image as a sensitive artist. Amy was the poet of amnesia, the actor in a play about emotional extinction.

A hollow person, unworthy of redemption.

A typical sunny afternoon in the Duran family den, with Isao sitting in front of the television and Gordon behind him on the couch saying nasty things, as usual.

"I wish you'd shut up," he said to Gordon, trying to watch *Laverne and Shirley*, his favorite show of all time. He ran home every day from the bus stop so he could snag a Dr. Pepper out of the fridge and watch another episode.

Daddy didn't like him watching much TV, didn't like much of anything now that he was staying home from work. He always complained that Isao and Gordon were a couple of lazy butts and they made too much noise.

The noise part was because of Gordon, who thought that being four years older than Isao meant he could play his stereo way too loud, talk on the phone all the time, and, worst of all, make fun of *Laverne and Shirley* for the way the girls always got into trouble.

"What a doof," Gordon said when Laverne rolled down the stairs. "Like I really believe someone would do that."

Since Mom wasn't back yet from visiting Mrs. Salgado next door, it would have to be Daddy to tell Gordon to shut up. Isao had to find Daddy so Gordon would spend the rest of the day in his bedroom. Served him right.

Isao ran up the stairs yelling for his father, skittered through his parents' bedroom, and stopped at the bathroom.

"Daddy?" he asked hesitantly. No answer.

Hearing a thump through the ceiling, he went to investigate. Daddy spent a lot of time in the attic. Laying down insulation, he said, though it seemed to be taking him forever. Opening a door in the hallway, Isao clambered up the stairs and, reaching the top, turned around and started to speak.

Daddy hung from the rafters, his face looking all purple.

Isao ran over and tugged on Daddy's leg, trying to wake him up, trying to get his attention, but nothing worked. Daddy just hung there like a tire from a tree.

Turning on his heels, Isao ran down the steps and into his room, slamming the door behind him.

I didn't see anything, he thought. I'm going to pick up all my clothes and put them in the dirty clothes hamper, and I'm going to do my homework. Daddy will be so proud of me, he'll give me a great big hug, and then he'll smile like he used to.

Isao next found himself in the den with a violin in his hands, which had been a gift from Mom's parents. Time to practice his solo; otherwise, Mrs. Szabo would pitch a fit the next time he went over for lessons. As he opened the sheet music, he heard Mom talking on the phone in the kitchen. She sounded tired.

"I don't want Pete in this house anymore, Mama. He can stay away forever, for all I care."

Isao tried not to move on the bench. He was afraid a sudden creak would give him away.

"That's not how it happened and you know it. You know Pete and I weren't seeing each other back then. All he did was drop by the house looking for a free meal, and Guillermo got upset. You know how he was toward the end, angry all the time. I don't feel guilty, Mama, I don't. Let Pete see that girl back home, be the big man for his friends. I'm sick of him."

Pete. Oh yeah, Mom's truck driver friend. He was at Daddy's funeral five years ago and came to see Mom when he was passing through town. He was a short, dark, Cajun man who always brought fresh boudain sausage iced down in his cooler, along with bottles of beer. Mom laughed a lot when he was around, seemed somehow younger.

"No, Mama. I don't want any part of him. Next time he calls, you tell him to quit coming by."

Getting up slowly from his chair, Isao went upstairs to the bathroom he and Gordon shared, and threw up lunch.

He had been getting too fat lately on Mom's cooking. He wasn't working hard enough on his homework and was only running a mile a day. Did he think magic was going to earn him an academic scholarship and a spot on the basketball team?

His daily shooting drills wouldn't help him survive tryouts next month, and as for his grades, he'd be lucky to make top five in his middle school graduating class. Isao had so much to do, all because he was so lazy he hadn't done it earlier.

Fast-forward to an early morning rainstorm, thunder muttering beyond his walls. Isao was slow to realize that the phone had been ringing for some time. Probably his girlfriend was calling to deliver another lecture on how Isao needed to eat more. Isao's girlfriend didn't have to live in this clumsy, lead-footed body, so weighed down by unnecessary poundage, by useless expectations.

An idiot, he was such an idiot to think he could teach teenagers to love literature when Twain was the last thing on their minds. About all he could control was his body, and that only fitfully, but lately he felt a change happening. Isao didn't have to throw up anymore, for the weight just fell off him.

Eating seemed so alien, like something dogs or cats did, not a fit occupation for a human being. There were times when he felt buoyant, lighter than air. He lived for those moments.

A lightning bolt burning the night sky, he rose reluctantly to close the curtains on the north window. He noticed during the next flash an apparition in the dressing table mirror.

Again, the sky lit up, and again he saw a frail stick of a creature with elongated limbs. Nosferatu's vampire, as seen in a funhouse mirror. Again, the lightning strobed. Oh God.

With that, Isao fell to the floor, flailed at righting himself, and then fell again. Adrenaline panic overwhelmed his defenses.

I'm dying, he thought. Oh God, help me. Help me. I can't go on like this.

AMY LIVED ISAO'S LIFE. SHE WAS ONCE ISAO, AND NOW AGAIN.

To be him was to be a highly decorated murderer, a dancer, a baseball junkie, a hopeless romantic, a commercial artist, an actor and singer, a man purged by war of all religious feelings, a man too easily controlled by others.

Isao felt Amy's emotions, was fully Amy in every respect.

To be her was to be a skilled yet untalented violinist, a runner, a basketball fan, a book lover, a converted Jew, a timid woman who rarely let anyone get too close, a woman who nearly starved herself to death.

Dusk approached.

Isao and Amy stood again in the rice paddy. Nearby, pale birds disappeared into a blurred metallic gold horizon. They were standing so close together, inside each other's breath, each other's thoughts.

"Why don't you hate me?" they asked.

"Because I understand you," they answered.

"There's no reason to hold back anymore," they said, tentatively.

"None."

"Who shall we be?" they asked.

No answer.

She sank into him. Isao pushed away, suddenly desperate as he felt a tugging toward her. At the periphery of his vision, a white bird flung itself into the sky and winged toward the western glow.

He felt Amy's embrace, her acceptance, and then all sensation faded.

A warm, humid place. Late evening. Somewhere in the distance, a low thumping sound rose in strength then faded, borne by a passing vehicle. The rumble of anxious voices, steady but not invasive.

Eyes closed, no need to open them. Rest. Rest.

FIFTEEN

I RUSHED TO AMY'S HOUSE, NOT EXPECTING TO SEE WHAT APPEARED TO BE A normal, sound slumber.

When she rolled over on her side, Amy—I hoped Amy—mumbled something in that language all sleepers share.

Rabbi Fleischer, his broad face betraying the tension of the moment, told me that Amy had immediately gone to sleep after Marin began her relaxation mantra. Amy experienced what appeared to be a nightmare before settling down.

Mike, who I'd called on the way over, had beaten me to the door, despite having been en route to the airport. I had talked him out of ordering an overnight shipment of beta-anodynol. He now was pacing in the backyard and smoking through a pack of cigarettes.

Marin sat smoothly self-contained and almost smug when she announced that she'd persuaded Isao to leave by Amy's higher self. Toni Akugawa, who had already left by the time I arrived, wasn't answering her cell phone.

"What's Amy doing now?" Nina asked Marin skeptically.

"Sleeping. She's had a very difficult time of it. I'm sure she'll have quite a story for us when she wakes up."

We gathered around the kitchen table, working on cups of coffee and trying to keep our voices down.

Gordon and Randall were en route to Amy's house from attending a baseball game in Houston. Nina reported that Gordon sounded furious when he learned about the ad-hoc regression.

Nina posted herself at the doorway and said to Marin, "Why don't you stop yapping about higher selves and pay attention to the person who's right in front of you."

I told Marin that I didn't appreciate that she'd left me out of the planning.

She let out a trill of laughter. "You shouldn't be so possessive, Carla. Amy needed a holistic experience, which is beyond the scope of your practice."

"No offense, Dr. Marin, but Amy saw you as a facilitator and nothing more," Rabbi Fleischer said with an air of quiet conviction. "She thought your technique would be useful in getting started, but what she and I prayed for was healing and understanding. I know she believes that Isao is her past life—"

"Which is the truth," Nina broke in. "None of y'all want to believe it. Maybe it isn't according to Saint Buddha or the Bible, but it's what she thinks." She turned her head back to the living room. "Oh, she's awake."

We decamped for the living room where a tired-looking Amy sat on the sofa.

When I asked her how she felt, she silently rose and walked out onto her patio. We trailed behind her like aides to a lifetime senator. The scent of violets wafted through the late night air. She stared out expressionless at a sky reduced by city glare to a bare sprinkle of stars.

Mike, now seated on a lawn chair, held an unlit cigarette in his hand. He looked miserable.

Nina touched her on the shoulder and offered her a glass of water. Amy took it with an almost imperceptible bow.

Rabbi Fleischer stood by the patio table, his cup of coffee still in hand. Marin had an elated expression on her face.

For the moment, Dr. Turner, a dispassionate clinician, had the floor.

The question had to be asked. "Who are you?"

She rubbed her eyes and yawned, regarding me with an expression at once sorrowful and musing.

"Amy was stuck in a crowded house; Isao couldn't leave. They were the same soul, the same book, just different pages. Isao raped and killed, killed with a patriotic pride, he thought, and then he went on to live a normal life until he couldn't stand being himself anymore. That's why he became an actor, so he could pretend to be other people, people who hadn't committed terrible acts. Amy was the one who actually tried to kill herself. She did it the slow way, but that's what it amounted to."

Isao, Amy? Someone new. Speaking with a boldness and fluidity of emotions in her face I had never seen in either of the previous residents, yet filtered through a Japanese accent.

I heard Marin clearing her throat to my left, preparing to bring down her prey.

Amy walked over to a tearful Nina.

"Amy never opened up to another human being all the time she was alive. She had good friends, dear friends, a family she adored, a therapist she cared about. She never let any of them in, because that would have meant letting herself remember seeing her father dangling from a handmade noose."

Unable to contain her reaction, Nina gathered Amy into an embrace that seemed to comfort Nina more it did Amy, but it lasted for a long moment, allowing Marin her entry.

"Who's here now? Amy or Isao?" Marin asked.

"Just let it play out, Faye, let it play out. There's nothing you can do about it now," Mike said softly.

Amy turned to look at us all, her gaze stopping on me. "There was only one solution. I didn't want it. You couldn't allow yourself to see it, but it was there all the time."

I stated the obvious. "To join the two camps. Integrate your dual consciousnesses."

She gave me a sober nod and sat down on a patio chair. The casual strength of her moves somehow was the capper to her words. Flow, yet control.

I could hear Nina gasp behind me.

Marin said in a low tone, "Bullshit."

"Amy." Rabbi Fleischer gazed at her beseechingly. "Or Isao, or whatever I should call you, you're saying you're one person now, but how can that be? Two spirits—"

"One. There was only one all along," the woman with Amy's face said.

Mike got up and left, not saying a word.

Gordon and Randall arrived just as Amy, or whoever was in there, had been helped to bed. Nina volunteered to take the first shift in watching over her.

I reluctantly agreed to talk to Marin out on the patio.

She wandered over to the nearest flowerbed, bent down, and examined a chrysanthemum. "You know, it takes a patient person to maintain a garden this beautiful. Someone who's strong-willed and stubborn."

"Your point?"

"She's still in there. Isao's gained the upper hand for now. Amy may be in abeyance, but her Higher Self remains available. Come on, Carla, you gave her an experimental drug and confused her so much that another spirit came calling. Don't try to tell me that little mouse can rewrite the Vedas, negate thousands of years of progressive enlightenment, and claim she has somehow crazy-glued two lives together. Don't tell me that."

Marin refused to accept that this breakthrough came sans her belief system and definitely sans Marin. She saw this as a turf battle and me as her enemy.

Finally understanding that, I reached a level of calm I hadn't felt in weeks.

When she began rat-a-tatting the same old points, I went back into the house where I found a bleary-eyed Gordon and Randall sitting around the kitchen table. Someone—probably Randall—had gone on a beer run. I joined father and son in knocking down our bottles of Shiner Bock.

This was not a night for lectures, not by anyone for any reason. A couple of minutes later, we heard the front door slam as Marin made her exit.

"Ding-dong, wicked witch," Randall said.

S I X T E E N

SHE WOKE UP THINKING ABOUT LYNDI, AN ASSOCIATE MANAGER AT WATERLOO
Records Amy dated for a time. Lyndi sported a beautiful tattoo of a Siberian tiger
on her forearm, and she'd talked about adding more endangered species.

From a certain angle, the tiger seemed to snarl in mid-leap, something of a
distraction during sex, but that wasn't the reason she and Amy stopped seeing
each other back in February. No, like previous girlfriends, Lyndi asked only that
Amy be open about her feelings.

Isao had been more expressive during his life. What about when that girl,
something Sumiko, brushed up next to Isao in the street? Like a fool, he'd blurted
out that she had the most beautiful eyes, which she did. When she laughed at him
and called him a *mobo*, didn't he from that point on try to dress and act like the
wildest boys in school?

And suddenly crazy for the tango, the samba, anything with a Latin beat, he'd
tried to make his hair flop into his eyes just like the dancer pictured in *Shimbun
Asahi*. Or dancing like the American, Fred Astaire, with the blonde woman. Isao
imagined dancing with Sumiko, imagined doing much more than that, but she
hardly noticed him after the incident in the street.

She lay in bed and watched the sun come up over the honeysuckle as she
listened to Nina sleeping in her chair. Someone had dressed Amy in a nightshirt.
She thought about trying to slip out of the room. As though reading her mind,
Nina woke up with a start, stalling her plans at raiding the closet for clothes.

Nina stretched and yawned, sneaking a peek at her in the process. Her
disappointment was obvious, though expressed more between the lines. "What

am I supposed to call you? Amy or Isao?"

She thought about it. "Call me Luz." Amy's middle name.

Carla came in, closely followed by Gordon, neither of them saying anything. They stared at her expectantly. Seeing Amy's brother made her think of Koichii. Jiro Endo said that Isao's brother had died decades ago. Not surprising, considering his heavy smoker's cough. She leapt into a fierce embrace with Gordon, the brother Amy had, a brother who seemed surprised by her action.

"Are you okay? Are you feeling better?" he asked.

"I'm feeling excellent, without a doubt. Hungry, and stinking, and needing to pee. I want to clean up before any question and answer sessions. Excuse me."

Luz bounded into the bathroom where she instantly noticed that the toilet was too close to the shower and tub. Talk about unhygienic. The shower and tub combo was all wrong with no place to sit down and do a good scrub, while the tub itself was nowhere near deep enough. She settled on a hot shower and hoped to have time later for a prolonged soak.

When she came out of the bathroom, Nina, all in a fidget, sat on her bed, alone.

"Okay. I need to understand what's going on here. How much of you is still Amy, and who do you think you are now? Please, help me on this."

As Nina spoke, Carla reentered the room.

E-mails from Amy's friends had piled up for weeks. Her co-workers at Bookish had been kept at arms length lately. What was she supposed to say to everyone?

The good mood she had been in vanished, even though she felt no more Other in her thoughts, only the blessed, unconfused I, First-person Singular, Controller of her Destiny. No longer half-and-half, *inoko.*

Lightly, brightly, into this new millennium, God or chance had given her, yet it weighed on her that whomever she told about this might tell others. They couldn't help it. The word would get out at some level that somewhere lived the first truly enlightened one. Or a demon.

It would be equally bad back in Tokyo. The priests would march against an upstart woman who threw karma out the window, who unearthed her past life and decided to keep it as a perverted sort of necrophilia. She'd been living in a cocoon. Maybe she could keep her name quiet by relying on patient's privacy rights. But someone could put it on the Net, which would drag everyone she'd ever known into an *arashi* only a tornado could top.

Everyone from Isao's immediate family was dead, except for his son, Masao. When Isao was a dead man existing due to another's tolerance, he deliberately put any thought of Masao out of his mind. And now? Jiro Endo said that Isao's son was alive.

Her son. The phrase alone unsettled her, let alone the reality of an elderly man who might still harbor memories of a father who took him to backstage rehearsals. *Shichigo-san.* How could she have ever suppressed memories of taking Masao to the local shrine? His eyes lit up at the chance to ring the giant bell. A shy, exquisite boy, so unlike these boisterous American children. Masao.

I SAW HER EYES FILL WITH MOISTURE, AND OVERFLOW. SHE STILL HAD NOT uttered a word until she whispered "ee-yay." The Japanese word for no, one of the words I had taught myself in the past few weeks.

If she said anything more in Japanese, what could I do? Next to nothing without translation by Toni, who had retreated into her faith, fearful of blasphemy. My faith had proven to be all too shallow.

The sadness in this woman's face was grief unmediated by the distancing measures she had relied upon all her life. I knew now that I could have cared for Amy fifty years and, if not for a dead man's intervention, never have known the truth about her father's suicide. So, how real had been my affection? To love—admit the truth now—to love someone who hid so much of herself from me could be nothing more than heightened empathy.

I called her by the name her brother had provided. Her face, livened for a moment by seeing me, became tense.

"Tell me about Masao."

Gordon walked in as I answered.

"Masao is retired and living with his oldest son in Seattle. He's a widower and has several grandchildren."

I told Luz what little I knew from talking to Mike. Masao Watanabe worked in the diplomatic field for many years before his retirement. His son was the second highest-ranking official at the Japanese consulate in Seattle. He handled some trade matters but seemed to be more of a cultural attaché. Both Watanabes were fluent in English and the son, Akira, held a graduate degree in foreign affairs from Georgetown University. Seattle was but one stop in his advancement up the diplomatic ranks.

She stirred at the end. "I want to see him."

Slouched in a chair in the corner, Gordon shook his head. "I can understand why you'd want to see Isao's son. Hell, you have every reason to, but he doesn't know you from Adam, and you have a lot of things to work through here."

Something about Gordon's attitude had changed, but it took me a minute to pin it down.

"Don't forget, you've missed so much work lately," Nina said.

"Yeah, give it time," Gordon said. "How's he going to take meeting you if you're still shaky from all the stuff that's gone down? Give it time."

With those words from her brother, I realized the difference. Gordon was now responding to the androgynous cues given out by Luz. He treated her with a rough-edged affection, doing it with an ease that surely masked more conflicted emotions. She nodded in agreement, not pleased with the advice, but on the surface willing to delay a trip to the West Coast.

Later, over breakfast, I watched Luz hash a fried egg into her rice and eat the mess with gusto as she peppered Randall's description of a recent baseball game with questions about various players. She acted more lively than the rest of the table, although Nina tried to match Luz's energy level.

A lull in the conversation. I realized from Nina's solemn expression that I'd missed something important.

Luz shrugged. "I can't tell you where Isao leaves off and Amy starts. I don't know the answer to that one, but I do know I feel alive right now. Vivid, screaming alive, like I've been in sepia all these years and someone finally clicked the color button. I know some of you think Isao was a ghost. You'll never believe otherwise. But I'm telling you, he was as real as Amy."

Nina looked overwhelmed. The Durans, both father and son, were doing only slightly better at hiding their emotions.

I thought I could bring Amy back from the nether world and alter a scenario that had never been in my power to control. Now she sat before me, bold and confident, even her hair combed a little differently. Time to let go of that reserved woman, the Amy I had grown to love. She wasn't coming back this time.

SEVENTEEN

CARLA SEEMED MELANCHOLIC THROUGHOUT THE MEAL, NOT REACTING TO LUZ'S efforts at humor. She left without saying much more than goodbye. Nina at least was more effusive, promising to call her later in the day, leaving only Gordon and Randall, who sat expectantly in the living room.

Randall led off. "So, like, do you think you're a man or a woman?"

"I can't forget my gender, now can I?"

Gordon delivered a frown in Randall's direction, which had the desired effect.

Gordon began squinting, a sure sign he was trying not to cry. "I'd been ready to spend the rest of my life trying to learn Japanese, so having you back to any degree is a blessing.

"When Dr. Turner told me you finally remembered that day in the attic, I knew you'd taken some hard hits last night. Yet, you didn't leave again. You hung in there, and I want you to know I'm very, very proud of you. The thing I'm worried about is how all this is going to affect you. You want to find your son, even though I don't see him ever believing your story. Also, I've been thinking about what Dr. Turner told me: Borlauch wants to do more research on this kind of thing. I don't think you should deal with them."

"Don't worry, I won't," Luz said.

"What if this gets out on the Net?" Randall jumped in excitedly. "We were so worried about you we didn't really think about it, but you know, that Zilinsky guy was recording the whole thing. Some major shit's gonna come down over this. Dad and I were talking—"

"Randall, shut up," Gordon said.

"About what to do if the vultures come around—"

"I mean it, Randall."

Chastened, Randall sat mutely as Luz thought it over. "Okay, what's your plan?"

Her brother mumbled something under his breath at Randall, then regrouped. "Okay, I've been talking to Miguel down in Monterrey. You remember my old college buddy, I hope. You know he's been after me to work with him. He's made full professor, and he's opened an art gallery on the side, which he wants me to run. Hell, you're trilingual now, though your Spanish could use a lot of work. There's bound to be a demand for people who translate for tourists and businesses."

She let him continue in that vein a while longer and told him that she'd think it over.

Randall looked unhappy as they left. He whispered in her ear, "I've got your back, no matter what."

If they could save her, she'd let them do it, but was that even possible? Later in the day, she went up to Bookish and handed in her resignation in a meeting that her boss dragged out to the parking lot before giving up.

She hadn't a clue what she said to him. Something brisk and to the point, which was not at all the way she felt. Amy had a good job, but that woman left last night arm in arm with Isao, leaving behind their memories, their desires, and their attributes. She couldn't imagine working in a *honya* all day, faced with boring book shipments and author anxieties. How mundane—wings scraping against the window desperate for escape. She'd be *baka yaro* for sure; take her back to Brackenridge.

Luz stopped at Central Market. She bought several jars of pickled Japanese fruits and vegetables along with rice crackers, soba noodles, plastic containers of miso and tofu, fresh-ground Jamaican coffee, a tube of wasabi, ginger root, Chilean wine, plum tomatoes, rice vinegar, bok choy, red bell peppers, jalapeños, basmati rice, green onions, pinto beans, a six-pack of Cokes, peanut oil, and potato salad. She would have bought more items except that along about the cheese section she realized she was buying for two people when she only had one stomach and one refrigerator, for that matter.

Groceries put up, reassuring phone-calls made, she headed for her computer, where she drank a beer and nibbled on crackers while she made changes in her resume. None of it distracted her from a blinding headache.

Gordon had pointed out that she was trilingual. However, Isao frequented Chinese restaurants in part to improve his schoolboy Mandarin and in part because he loved the cuisine. He always thought he was fluent in Mandarin.

She pulled out a copy of Toni Morrison's *Beloved* and stumbled through translating a paragraph into Mandarin. She could get by on talking a lot better than she could on reading the language. Big deal. If she worked her butt off, she could market herself as a four-language—what was the word, quadralingual?—specialist. Or maybe lead off with her best asset.

She stared at the page, her mind's voice shifting from Japanese to English then back again with equal ease. If only her word-processing program worked that effortlessly. It was time to take some ibuprofen before going online.

She ordered a Japanese-language keyboard and software, along the way downloading programs that would allow her browser to correctly render Japanese and Chinese characters.

During a visit to a Japanese tanka site, she thought again about checking her e-mail and text messages. There had to be a ton piled up.

No. She needed to keep the truth to as small a circle as possible. Someone with Borlauch or the hospital might out her at any point. Why make it easy for them?

EIGHTEEN

I TOOK THE GIRLS ON A CAMPING TRIP IN LATE AUGUST. WE RAFTED AND CAMPED in Big Bend Park, slept under the stars, and sweltered under the sun.

I tried not to think about anything important, just paddling around a bend in the river, rock formations high above our heads. After a while, even Rashida, accustomed to nonstop texting and tweeting, spent more time paying heed to nature than missing her invisible chorus.

Every day Imani surprised me, once by calmly plucking an ant off her trail mix before eating it, the trail mix, not the ant, and another time by not crying when I pulled cactus needles out of her leg, although her eyes grew into saucers upon seeing a two-inch specimen. Growing up, emotionally and literally, she towered over me. She stood a shade over six-foot-one, and the doctor said she still had some growing to do.

Rashida, smaller and more worldly-wise, had also changed over the summer. She was quieter, more tolerant. By way of Randall, whom she was seeing—tell the truth, she was using more than her eyes with him—I learned how Luz was handling her integrated life. I learned the details second-hand, for I had decided not to continue a professional relationship.

I signed a letter to her not long after the merge that gave suggestions on who to call if she needed to restart therapy. Rashida's advice, unsolicited, consisted of me asking Luz for a date, which struck me as a terrible idea. Why would this new construct have any feelings for me?

We all came back refreshed and renewed, and the girls flung themselves into their classes with a vigor that surprised me. Rashida changed her major from

English literature to psychology. She also signed up for a course in beginning Japanese.

A couple of weeks after vacation, Mike e-mailed me saying that the first formal test of what he dubbed the Borlauch past-life protocol would take place at the end of the month in Chicago. Would I attend?

Marin had somehow wangled an invitation. Dr. Nyanga no doubt took the measure of the woman and knew Marin would earn them tremendous publicity— if the procedure worked.

Marin promised anonymity for Luz. Anonymity for the doctors involved? Unlikely. Like it or not, I'd made myself into an apparent knockoff of Faye Marin. That was a depressing thought.

IT HAD BEEN FUN WATCHING THE EXCITING COWBOYS GAME AT THE BAR, EVEN with the Cowboys' mistakes making them struggle for the win. Ben Stovall, on the losing side, paid for another round. Feeling a nudge in her side, Luz heard Ben advise her to check out the bar. She saw a petite Asian woman sitting alone.

"She's been staring at you the past fifteen minutes," he said.

The femme was pretty, with bold eyes.

"I don't know her."

"Silly girl, she wants to know you, and she might even be Japanese."

They'd had this conversation before about other *koshoku* objects. Ben tried to create meet-ups whenever a possible lover appeared. She still felt an indefinable strangeness at the thought of touching anyone.

Isao possessed the romantic looks that drew female admirers and, upon reflection, certain men into his orbit, yet he never once cheated on a wife who proved to be faithless. Women to him were wonderful creatures with many worthy attributes, but not, for all that, his equals.

Amy, on the other hand, might have had a more realistic view of relationships but still liked her partners to be on the butch side. She enjoyed being pursued, being courted.

Each of them had a streak of old school mores.

Luz turned around in her chair to face the woman and smiled.

Tracy Hara, an IT specialist, turned out to be a good conversationalist. She was attractive and could even speak Japanese, filtered through her strong Texas accent. But despite the woman's many charms, Luz couldn't keep the conversation afloat, even with Ben doing his best subverbal prodding. She foundered on the simplest of flirtations. They ended the encounter only exchanging phone numbers.

Afterward, coffee brewing in Luz's kitchen, Ben said earnestly, "You could buy something if you need a certain length to, you know, get in the mood. Maybe that's all you need."

"That's your wishful thinking," Luz said with a laugh. "Get yourself an extra six inches and see if the men line up for you. I don't need a tool chest."

"Excuse me." Ben feigned being insulted. "Oh, I just remembered I got a text message from Dr. Jiro Endo today. He asked about you."

"What did you tell him?"

"That you're doing well. Are you?"

Later, alone on the patio, she drank her coffee and inhaled the night air in equal amounts. Had it been only three months ago that she made her debut in front of Carla and the others, to all appearances a freak blend of two worn-out, screwed-up lives? Good riddance to all of that.

Since then, she had left Bookish and taken a part-time translator position at Regala, a textbook publisher in town. She added, through Ben's connections, occasional translation/guide work with Japanese tourist groups. Regala might be moving her into permanent hire, if that was what she wanted to do with the rest of her life. If she even knew what she wanted to do.

Earlier, Nina called her about a mysterious mention in the *Austin Chronicle* of unusual experiments going on at a local hospital. A raised eyebrow piece that offered no further details. Luz had doubts about her long-term chances of remaining undetected. She did talk Gordon out of his plans to move all of them to Monterrey. She saw no point in him uprooting his entire life to try to protect his little sister.

The next morning, Luz's senior editor called her into his office. It was a lightly furnished closet with a pile of boxes in the corner. Frankly, she felt envious. He told her in his usual restrained twitch that she was being promoted to junior assistant editor, full-time, with benefits, plus a raise, "but don't expect a bigger cubicle just yet."

Perhaps she took too long to digest the news. He blinked rapidly. "Believe me, you deserve a bigger raise than that, but you haven't been here six months yet."

Barely three months. "I take it that you're pleased with my job performance."

"Oh yes, oh yes. Well, at first, we were concerned with the speed of your translations."

"I'm new to this kind of work. I am getting faster."

Maximum blinkage. "Oh no, it's that you were turning in the chapters so quickly. We double-checked some of it with a very reputable translator. You see, we had six months of projects backed up, which was one reason for hiring you part-time. Ikeda Publishers wants to go full-speed on our partnership, and it's the work of people like you who have made it possible."

Ikeda? Amy had once booked an in-store appearance by one of their novelists, considered a leading figure in the new opaque-realism movement.

"I thought Regala only did textbooks."

The blink festival again. Her editor went into a lengthy explanation of the two publishers wanting to expand their international horizons, cross-market convergence, blah blah blah. Nothing but words to avoid pointing out how important she had become to their scenario.

Jigoku no sata mo kane shidai, or as Ben would say, money talks, bullshit walks. She cleared her throat to signal an end to his diversionary tactics.

"Tell you what. Double my salary, and I'll stay on here. Your pay stinks, but I wanted to give you a chance to see what I can do. I want to stay in Austin. It's a beautiful town with the loveliest blossoms on its trees, but I've been thinking about relocating to the West Coast."

The West Coast reference had its intended effect. By the end of the day, her promotion morphed from junior assistant editor into assistant editor. Her editor readily agreed that she could do much of her work at home. Why not? It was her electricity and her computer. Why wouldn't they approve?

All this for a job she hadn't taken seriously. She hadn't bothered to bone up on Regala's corporate history, research being an Amy trait if there ever was one. Work was work. Start every morning where you left off yesterday. There is a word or phrase for everything, she thought, even when the languages don't quite match in meaning. One only had to dig deeper to find it.

Although Isao had read little more than poetry and scripts, the richness of his life experiences gave him a huge vocabulary, while Amy possessed the discipline and literary background to apply their joint expertise.

Was this all it amounted to? Isao's awakening and the merging of their consciousnesses? Did it mean nothing more than being able to name her price as a translator? How mundane.

Rabbi Fleischer viewed her as a cultural and spiritual link between East and West, yet despite his invitation to return to services, she felt too knotted up with questions that God had yet to answer. No clouds had rolled away. The mystery remained unsolved.

Nothing resonated within her, not even the Shinto and Buddhist doctrines Isao had grown up with and later abandoned during the war. Religion and piety had become so much sludge in the gears to her, giving no traction to her course, no meaning to this impossibility.

The night a *pika* flash lit up Amy's skeletal body in the mirror, it caused her to see what she was doing to herself. At that moment, she experienced a breakthrough in which God reached out to her. That epiphany led to Carla and everything else that happened.

Where was God now? Maybe this conduit of energy she rested on, all the conduits, represented the whole of human existence. Sentient light, spirit lasers.

Dear Gordon, doing his best to help, called almost every day and sometimes went out with her and Ben. He still seemed to be channeling his former role as her surrogate parent. Gordon quit going to church years ago.

She couldn't talk to him about God. He did believe in her sanity, didn't believe that a vengeful Japanese *kami* possessed her body.

Amy's mother worshipped the Trinity, Mother Mary, the Holy Roman Church, every bit of it. She took her children to mass every time the door opened, until the day Father Mungia offered to pray for her husband's soul in purgatory, the traditional place for Catholic suicides. Offended, she never went back.

Amy sometimes missed the presence of her parents in her daily life—a father gone by her seventh birthday, her mother dead of cancer before her twenty-first. Their advice, condemnation, love, or indifference would have helped to ground her in this world. Now, detached from so much of that former life, Luz wondered what still mattered to her.

Isao's son, Masao, who, from all accounts, lived happily in Seattle. He didn't know and likely would never believe that his father, however transfigured, still lived.

Who else? Gordon and Randall. Nina. Ben, undemanding to a fault. Everyone else she held at a distance, whether locally or via the Internet.

Once upon a time, Amy thought she loved Carla, the warm buzz of her voice, the gentle inquisitiveness of her face. How much time did Amy spend considering the wide plane of Carla's cheekbones? She had been the locus of Amy's life, not that the patient ever said word one to the doctor on that subject.

What did Carla mean to Luz now, crossing through her mind like an errant kite on a wind current? Carla was a blossom Luz wanted to possess and cherish in equal measure.

Nina said the other day that Luz had simply morphed into a soft butch. Whatever the label, Luz almost upended one of her closest relationships one night at a club. Nina lived in the neighborhood of "don't go there," a fact underscored when Luz applied her less than skillful flirtations to Nina. She guffawed through Luz's spiel and the following apology.

According to group opinion, Luz needed to take on the social scene gradually. Slow and easy were not words that applied to her feelings about Carla.

NINETEEN

HMM. A JOHNSON PAINTING POSTED ONLINE FOR A PRICE NOT ALTOGETHER outrageous. Then again, that new artist, Ngeli Suwanga, had a more affordable piece. Art was my annual birthday present to myself and with it only a few weeks away, best to order now. I clicked on Suwanga, filled out the order form, and pressed enter.

I moved on to the CNN site, where I'd been keeping track of the riots in Algeria. An old schoolmate with whom I corresponded lived in Algiers, still unable to obtain a visa to the United States. Although I agreed to be a sponsor, the embassy there remained indifferent to the plight of a gay intellectual caught up in the latest anti-Western backlash. The phone rang. I listened to the answering machine click on.

"Carla, this is Luz. Are you busy Friday night? Let's go out. Seven-thirty is fine. Let me know. Bye."

I played it back, unable to believe my ears. Though I heard a trace of Isao's accent, much of Amy's voice had returned, yet without its tentativeness.

I called her back.

"Are you okay on the time?" she asked after I said hello.

"Sure."

"I'll pick you up. I know a great place to eat. Be ready to dance."

"Are you doing okay?"

Her voice kept its rapid pace. "I'm doing great. No complaints here."

"I want to apologize for not calling you. Things just got overwhelming."

There was a long pause before Luz spoke. "That's the first time you've ever spoke human to me," she said softly. "I didn't think you knew the language. I'll see you Friday."

The next two days I zipped through a packed schedule that included a long phone-call from Mike. He again insisted that I attend next week's experiment in Chicago.

He said it would relieve his tension to know that a friend was there to provide support. I was a friend, however, who refused to be actively involved in the session, a friend who opposed the entire concept of attempting to control a past-life regression. I saw too many variables and far too potent a profit motive for many of the participants.

Even so, he was right. If he disappeared the way Amy had, a woman who essentially never made it back, I would see my old friend for the last time.

I did not intend to examine my motives for seeing Luz. She wanted to see me, for whatever reason. According to Nina, Luz had changed almost beyond recognition, in ways Nina was reluctant to discuss. But Rashida had no compunctions.

"She's a party girl, going out all the time. She's all about dancing and drinking. Randall says all she's doing is enjoying life. But you'd think she just got out of prison the way she acts. She's real friendly, though."

"What about—"

"Mama, don't worry. I haven't seen her be romantic with anybody."

By the time Friday night came around, Rashida had spirited Imani over to a friend's house for a sleepover, while Rashida told me somewhat mysteriously that she had made her own arrangements.

"You better be careful now. Don't be getting into anything you can't handle tonight," I told her.

"Pot. Kettle. Black."

A few minutes after eight, Luz arrived, acting so ill at ease, I thought she would turn around and leave at the door. Wearing amethyst slacks and a filmy white top, she managed the social pleasantries better than I.

What was the evening supposed to accomplish, why were my palms so sweaty, and why did she look so jumpy, too? She still had an effect on me, when even the way her arms stretched out on the sofa betrayed an alien, masculine influence.

"You're wondering why the hell I came over tonight." Frank words, anxious eyes.

"I guess I am."

"Not a day goes by I don't think about you."

"And what is it that you think about me?"

A fleeting smile. "I'm not your patient anymore. Ready to roll?"

We followed a spicy meal of chicken and plantains at Tropicalismo with a stroll down Sixth Street. She made a point of stopping at a shop to examine the tattoo designs.

"There he is."

She angled her head at a young Asian man I recognized from the night Isao emerged. He was helping a ghost-white girl with pitch-black hair select a tongue stud. He raised his head and smiled at Luz.

"Hey, dude. Here to get a tat?" he asked.

"Just window shopping."

"That's cool."

While we walked out, she whispered, "I came in with Ben when he got a tat, and I swear he thought I was a man. There I was, wearing shorts and a wife-beater, and the whole time he called me sir."

I stopped in front of the store, forcing passers-bye to form currents around us.

"You're showing me your new life. Am I supposed to give you my blessing or turn and run? What am I supposed to do? What is it that you want from me?"

WAS CARLA THAT CLUELESS? CONFIDENT THAT CARLA WOULD FOLLOW HER, LUZ headed for her favorite dance club, where the bouncer at the door gave her a genial smile.

"Here to dance, *mi corazon*?" he said.

"All night, *mijo*, all night."

By the time she reached the dance floor, Carla caught up to her. Time to lead a workout. A salsa beat thumping through the speakers, she allowed Carla to think she was leading for a few minutes, until an agile Arab boy showed up. Soaked with perspiration, Carla went off to find a table.

The Arab boy had no problem with Luz leading him around the dance floor, nor did his successor, an older white woman whose name Luz was unable to hear over the din.

She did hear the woman say, "You're a great dancer," as Luz led her through some complex moves. Of course, she was good. She couldn't help but be good with so many years of practice. The beat changing over to retrodisco, they adjusted to the rhythm just as Carla arrived to reclaim her spot.

"You lead," Carla yelled.

Carla turned out to be not half-bad as a partner, though a bit too tall for spins. On a break, Luz watched the doctor knock down a screwdriver without pause and call over the waitress for another. It felt odd, looking at the woman now, and seeing not Amy's savior, nor Isao's scary judge, but an ordinary person with a case of nerves.

ON THE WAY OUT, BOTH OF US KNEW THROUGH DATE-OSMOSIS THAT WE WERE ready to leave. The bouncer came over and gave Luz a bear hug.

"Dude, you're looking sharp tonight," he said.

"See," she said as we walked to her car. "He thinks I'm a guy, too."

"I don't see how. What gives transsexuals away are the forearms, which are usually too big for a woman. You're proportioned correctly."

What a lame way to tell Luz that she looked incredible. I, on the other hand, was a loaded, sweat-stained mess.

"And how would you know?"

"I've been to drag shows, and I have a client who's transitioning."

She took me by the hand and led me around human roadblocks until, on a side street close by the parking lot, I let go of her hand. She looked back at me, puzzled.

"Are you okay?"

"You go out all the time?" I asked her.

"At first. It'd been so long since I'd gone dancing."

"A lifetime."

She shrugged. "And a few months. They both liked to dance. Isao happened to be good at it."

Amy was dead. Dead. Leaving this beautiful, commanding... what? A clone? Call her a child who'd inherited some of her parents' traits.

Walking toward me, she gazed at me intently.

"Carla, I want to get to know you again. Amy may have only been your patient, but she knew a lot of things about you. Like your art collection, for one thing, which to judge from what little I saw of your home, is nice. I know a bit about your time in the Army, your kids. You never said much about your wife, but you didn't have to. It must have almost destroyed you, losing her the way you did."

"I'd really rather not talk about her, if you don't mind."

A light rain had begun to fall.

"A psychologist who doesn't want to talk? How unusual." Fired at point blank, her aggressive stance was another reminder of Amy's absence. "Forgive me for being too personal, Dr. Turner."

A quiet ride home, unsurprisingly. Neither of us felt moved to comment on the sudden rain, or the traffic, or anything else. There, in my driveway, she tugged at my sleeve to keep me from getting out.

"Wait for the rain to clear."

Slipping in a CD, she cued a melancholic tune about plastic trees.

"Was that a favorite of Amy's?"

"No. She wasn't into classic Radiohead." Turning her face toward me, I saw the tears and realized she'd been crying for some time. "I guess I thought we could go out, and everything would be the way it should have been."

"What do you mean?"

"*Ai wa fumetsu nari.* Love is indestructible. It stands up to anything. Time. Death. I still love you."

Her voice broke at the end, and she turned her head away. Intending to comfort, I reached out to touch her shoulder and felt the muscles tense under my hand. Tense, then relax.

She ran inside with me as the rain pelted down, drenching us thoroughly before we reached the front hall. Did I notice the wildness in her eyes? Did I interpret it as desire? Did it matter?

I took a towel from a bathroom shelf and started drying us both off, but Luz took the towel from me and tossed it aside.

LUZ GRABBED THE TOWEL AND THREW IT SOMEWHERE—WHO CARED WHICH direction—not when Carla's body was right there in front of her, begging for attention. Luz saw her duty and went for it.

Luz took Carla on a jaunt down the hallway. Carla had to redirect them to the right door as she led them to the bed. Clothes off in a flash, Luz climbed on top and went to work and moments later, stopped in utter confusion. Carla felt so soft, as natural as a Basho haiku. Luz enjoyed putting her lips in all the places Amy imagined, but Amy had wanted something different, something more romantic than an Isao-style actioner. As for the woman who just now cried in the driveway—where was she?

"Baby, what's wrong?" Carla asked.

Damned if Luz knew, but she wasn't about to derail the night.

"Nothing at all. I'm just enjoying the ride."

I TRIED TO GIVE AS GOOD AS I GOT, EVEN AS LUZ'S BODY, SLICK FROM THE RAIN, KEPT slipping out of reach. Her mood mercurial, I attempted to match the shifts back and forth. Sometimes she felt as close as my breath; other times, she was orbiting an outer planet.

We came together, or closer to the truth, at the same time in the same room.

Rolling away, she rose to her feet and got dressed.

"What are you doing? Why are you leaving?" I asked.

No answer. I followed Luz to the door, my words seemingly no more than white noise to her. She kissed me for the first time then ran barefoot out to her car.

She looked back before getting in the car. She had a curious expression on her face. Later, I finally understood that look. Nostalgia.

Who had I made love to? And was love too generous a word for what had occurred? Her tears reminded me of Amy, her laughter of Isao. Almond-shaped eyes and long, graceful hands. Steely grace on a dance floor and in bed.

It didn't matter that I'd severed our professional relationship. Amy trusted me for years to do the right thing, and tonight had been no different. Had Luz tried being with others in a search for normalcy? It never crossed my mind to ask, so intent I had been on reclaiming an idealized Amy. I'd ignored the real one, however transfigured, in front of me.

Once again, I proved how little I considered her best interest throughout this whole affair. Once again, I had failed her.

"Belle," I whispered. "Why aren't you here to save me from myself?"

TWENTY

LUZ CHURNED OUT A NOTE-PERFECT RENDITION OF AIKO TORIYAMA'S LATEST novel, *Gambatte Kudasai*, well ahead of schedule, despite taking the time to read his earlier works, including an English translation. The translator, described in the blurb as a respected academic, didn't get across the flavor of Toriyama's robust, often colloquial style. She wasn't about to let that happen on her watch.

The past several decades had added many phrases to the Japanese language, which at first sent her running to print and online sources. But nothing lately gave her trouble, not even Toriyama's lengthy e-mails listing the many slang terms that needed proper voicing in English. Toriyama didn't care if his book sounded dated in twenty years. He wanted it fresh, and he wanted it now. Easy enough to do at her present rate.

Checking her voice-mail, she listened to Carla deliver a halting apology for the events of last night. Although she didn't need to apologize, Luz didn't want to get back to Carla yet. What a bizarre night.

Luz decided she'd had enough of Toriyama's symbolic retelling of the Forty-Seven Ronin tale, set in a Yakuza-owned nightclub right before a giant earthquake. The opaque-realism movement struck her as nothing more than an excuse to write a story without a compelling lead character.

Time for a walk around the backyard.

Her stroll took her past rows of rose bushes, elaborate trellises along the fences, and a waist-high hedge along the back. Other flowers teemed along the hedge. They massed into a multihued assault upon the eyes that had brought Amy no tranquility. Each day delivered a new imperfection.

The yard was full of imperfections now. Everywhere, plants called out for trimming, weeding, and watering, which were pleas Luz intended to ignore for the most part. She planned to uproot the whole lot during the winter and begin work on a stripped-down garden.

A pond would be nice. Combed gravel, a winding path toward the middle, a shady tree. Would water lilies do well in Austin's weather? She'd find the answer online. It was therefore a question that could wait.

Last night solved nothing. Carla kept trying to touch her, which just about wrecked Luz's concentration. While both of them had gotten off, she couldn't describe it as a romantic night. Unless she planned to date her left hand hereafter, there had to be a better way of achieving intimacy besides launching a bushido-style assault. *Yoku nai.* With sex came the obligation to care. She ignored that duty last night, because she was so intent on taking the hill.

Poor Carla, caught in the crosshairs like a deer, thinking she should have chosen another route through the forest, when she was doomed from the moment she answered Luz's phone message.

On outings with Ben and Nina, Luz had no problem flirting with other women, even if Nina said she had all the finesse of a bag of hammers. During his singleton days, Isao had been quite the smooth operator, so she couldn't blame her current bluntness on him.

Maybe Isao and Amy hadn't quite melded on a deeper level. Still, not much time had passed since what Nina persisted in calling the Big Bang. Give it time, she thought. In the meantime, no more harassment of Carla.

Damn. The doorbell. She opened the door to find Dr. Jiro Endo standing there.

What Dr. Jiro Endo wanted to drink more than anything else, thank you, was a glass of water. He stuck to English despite her efforts at steering him to Japanese. Pleased at her efforts in translating Toriyama, he studied the original and her translation. He turned his head from the screen after some minutes to remark on her skill.

"Thanks," Luz replied. "I thought this line of work would be harder than it's turned out to be. My boss keeps saying other translators take more time. They're worried I'm missing something, but whenever they have someone check my translations, everything's okay. Why is that? I mean, not why the translations are okay, but why am I so good at it? I've been visiting Web sites of other translators, and some of them were bilingual from an early age. I don't know if they're as fast as me, though."

Jiro had a ruminating expression. "The difference with you, I think, is hardwiring. Our brains are plasticized before birth to handle many different languages, but early on, the brain hardwires into a less malleable pattern to favor the primary tongue. Pathways get shut down. You're bilingual, so your brain took in two languages from an early age."

"That's pretty common in Texas."

"And in Montreal, but the vast majority of us, bilingual or not, don't pick up a language when we're adults and make it sound first nature."

"What's even weirder is that my Spanish has improved, and I'm even getting better at Mandarin, which was something Isao found hard to get better at."

"I moved to Toronto as a teenager. My inner voice, my thinking's in English, but my tongue still doesn't handle certain sounds like a native. I'm fluent, not native. When Isao came, you dreamed his dreams, and then he dreamed yours. I think that's the metaphor your mind created to explain how the combined drug dosages reshaped your neural pathways. I wish your family had permitted your doctors to order the scans during your stay in the hospital. It would have given us a lot of info."

"The brain can't reshape like that. Can it?"

"Stroke victims can to a certain extent. Their survival depends on the brain finding new paths around damaged areas. Your brain's perfectly healthy. Isao's dreams became your own, his language yours. Japanese has overlaid your initial linguistic hardwiring. You know, I repeat, you *know* your languages better than maybe any other human alive. It wouldn't surprise me to learn that the blending of your two selves hasn't slowed your neural plasticity and that you're even adding more language pathways. That's one reason why we've begun researching the possible effect of beta-anodynol on certain brain functions and whether at a recurring dosage, it could mimic linguistically what you achieved in the sessions."

"You think this is all because of the drug?"

He shrugged. "Whether because of the three separate doses or because of the sessions, or both, or neither, we don't know. That's the whole reason for research. To answer questions we start out not knowing we need to ask."

They sipped their drinks in silence. The purpose of his visit finally hit her.

"You want me to go to Chicago so you can study me, so you can do the scans."

He nodded. "To help us with our research, yes. But whether or not you do that, you need to know that Mike Zilinsky has selected himself to be the first subject for a controlled test of beta-anodynol-enhanced regression."

The idiot. "You can't control it. Not that way."

"They think by having access to an auto-translator and, if they need it, to scores of human translators both at the test and by other means, that this will take care of any problems. They believe they can retain Michael's presence throughout the session."

"What are your thoughts?"

"I think it's worthwhile to try it again, but I'm not sure Mike knows what he's getting into. Will you come?"

"To the regression? They won't stop it because of me."

"That's not why I'm asking you to come."

TWENTY ONE

TRUE, IMANI'S BEST FRIEND'S MOTHER SAID SHE WOULD LOVE FOR IMANI TO STAY with them for a couple of days, but I hated not being able to explain the real reason for the trip. Especially when Imani asked why, Mama, couldn't she go to Chicago, too, and see Uncle Mike, especially since Rashida was getting to go?

No good answer for that one, except that Rashida, who knew what Mike was risking, announced that she would be going to see him. Period. I paid for the plane tickets and hotel rooms, but not without a sense of trepidation. Losing the old Amy still hurt like hell, especially in light of last week's dating demolition. Giving my daughter the opportunity to experience that level of anguish didn't strike me as a parental duty. It was more like something two friends would agree to experience, like a deathbed vigil.

Dr. Jiro Endo greeted us in the lobby of Borlauch's main building. We walked into a vast, wandering edifice that was all silvery bubbles and swooping slides on the outside, reassuringly bland in the interior except for the omnipresent foliage.

I knew from my research online that the company's founder believed strongly in the regenerative power of oxygen. Ivy, bougainvillea, ferns, and some other plants I couldn't identify enjoyed free rein throughout the facility, except in those labs where sterile conditions were necessary. It made for an exotic blend of corporate Americana and Amazonia.

According to Jiro, Borlauch's executive board had already committed millions of dollars to the project, not only for Mike's self-immolation, but also for slated experiments into the mutability of drug-enhanced learning. Still more lay ahead because a government agency had sent representatives to today's experiment.

Which agency, Jiro declined to specify.

Knowing full well who paid Jiro's salary, I still found it easy to trust him. I wondered what his views were on the implications of induced past-life retrieval, or for that matter, the scientific basis of reincarnation.

Batting aside my attempts to turn the conversation in that direction, he said simply, "This isn't about faith; this is about science. I can't help but believe, and I can't help but question."

We found Mike next door to the conference room in a small room crowded with feverish-eyed technicians, the elbow jam in part created by a pair of tall, sleek, black mainframes, while Mike himself looked cheerful, almost giddy.

"So, like, this stuff is to link up with the guys at Stanford, right?" Rashida asked.

Mike laughed too loudly, caught himself, then smiled.

"We skipped Stanford and went right to the source. IBM sent us their mainframes and the tech. All the software's right here. They worked a deal with Borlauch to retain exclusive rights when the large-scale study is approved. They'll be able to handle auto-translations from all over the country once they're hooked up. Guess what? Nyanga's doing the induction today. Talk about your heavy hitters."

I took his hand and looked at him firmly. "You can stop this. You can change your mind."

"It was my idea."

"It can be your idea to not do it," I insisted.

Shaking his head, he said in a soft voice, "I'm sorry, but I'm going through with this, no matter what. I'll be okay."

Tears streaming down her face, my daughter left the room before he finished speaking.

"Why are you doing this?" I asked.

"My sister asked me that. She's made the same points you have in your e-mails, but it's like I told her and what I'm telling you. Someone has to follow up on what happened in Austin. Might as well be me."

"No, it doesn't. Let someone else be the pioneer."

He erupted. "Carla, we both fucked up royally, but mostly it was me. I knew the drug was powerful. There's a man from one of the earlier studies who still doesn't eat meat, all because a researcher followed her own agenda. We fired her, but the damage had been done. You didn't know how tricky the stuff is. I did, and I still said yes. It's my fault we ruined her life."

I flashed back on the Luz of a week ago, vibrantly brash, so different from the gentle, refined woman who walked into the second session.

"She's not ruined, Mike. She's literally not the woman she used to be, but she seems happy."

As the techs attached a wireless microphone to his shirt, Mike said flatly, "She's made the best of it, but I'm going ahead with this."

WHERE HAD JIRO GONE, LUZ WONDERED AS SHE TOOK IN THE BRIGHTLY LIT conference room. It curved in a semi-circle around a raised platform. The patient would be sitting in a large leather chair. Already seats were filling up.

A blonde Borlauch official, who looked vaguely familiar, sat beside her and asked probing questions about the ins and outs of translating books and cultural differences between Japan and the United States. The questions were a bit tiresome, especially since the Asian woman sitting on her left seemed to be drinking it all in. So much for secrecy.

Her neighbor also looked familiar. That night at the bar with Ben, there was a woman who hit on Luz, and vice-versa. Tracy Somebody.

"She talks too much, doesn't she," Tracy remarked in fluent Japanese that came out with a California lilt. The Texas twang must have been her cover.

Luz responded in the same language. "Yes, she does. But you left out some details the last time we met."

Angered by the interruption, the sharp-faced official settled back in her chair.

"Yes, I did. I'm Tracy Hara. I'm from the government, and I'm here to help." Tracy gave her a broad grin. "A classic line, I know, but true in this case. I think the problem with your nosy neighbor is that she doesn't believe in you."

"I don't care what she believes. I'm not a god."

"I agree with you on the last part. As for what happened to you, I've seen the recordings and read the documentary evidence. I even flew to Japan to visit people who knew you."

"They're still alive?"

"I found Koiko—your brother, Koichii's, daughter—and a handful of other people. You're now a well-documented person, better than a number of bigger stars from that time. In fact, I created a Wiki page for you based on the research that's been done so far."

Isao was now on Wikipedia? How strange, Luz thought. "How's Koiko?"

"Expecting her third great-grandchild. She's doing well. I told her, I told all of them, that I'm doing my doctoral thesis on you. No one seemed to think it odd that I'm researching, forgive me, an obscure TV actor from the early '60s."

"That he was. Since I'm not Isao, it makes me uncomfortable to be called by his name." Luz switched to English mid-stride.

"He's a part of you. You can't deny that, Amy." Tracy made an equally seamless switch.

"Call me Luz. I don't know how to put it, but, Amy and Isao, they're not here anymore. There's just little old me rattling around inside."

She tried to put a lighter spin on it. Tracy seemed prepared to argue the point for hours if need be.

"Who are you then?" A woman's voice, pitched low, came from behind her. The voice and the face, instantly recognizable. Dr. Faye Marin. She was Carla's nemesis and, indirectly, the reason why everything had happened.

Luz had counted herself lucky that Marin didn't try to contact her after the merge. Her luck ran out.

Marin repeated the question.

Luz saw Carla and Rashida enter the auditorium accompanied by Jiro Endo, the only one of the three who didn't appear shocked to see her.

As they wound their way to the seats nearby, Luz spoke. "I don't have a simple answer for you."

Dr. Marin pounced. "You don't have any kind of answer. You don't want to face how much was lost during our session. Since this is Amy's plane of existence, she has a right to experience it free of interference from any past life."

Tracy interrupted. "You now believe Isao is a past life?"

Marin nodded grimly. "This so-called experiment promises us the chance to connect with the karmic life force that unites everyone in every state of existence. I say so-called, because Nyanga already knows it works. All of it is leading to this moment, the greatest paradigm shift in the history of humanity."

Carla seemed upset, as though she was about to challenge Marin at any moment, while Rashida wore that frosty look she used when Randall acted up one too many times. Rashida belonged back in Austin, keeping her boyfriend and Amy's nephew in line, but, apparently, Carla wanted her daughter to witness Mike Zilinsky's potential suicide.

Jiro Endo came closer, his face impassioned, yet free of anger.

"I also consider this to be a special moment, Dr. Marin," Jiro said quietly. "We differ on why."

"It seems to me that, since you're a Buddhist, you'd be pleased to have your views validated in a scientific study."

"This validates nothing in the tradition. I have studied their lives in detail, searching for karmic triggers, the required moments. There's nothing that qualifies."

Dr. Marin's eyes could have scorched asbestos. "What about the suicides?"

"Isao didn't kill himself. What's more, his return can't be justified in karmic terms. This is something completely new. This procedure allows us to gather our past lives. It gives us the potential to gain spiritual knowledge unavailable to us before."

"Satori," Tracy said.

"But, Jiro, I'm not an enlightened person," Luz said.

"Give it time. Both of your parents died young, and you're still a child."

She didn't have to ask to which parents he was referring.

He took her hand. "Allow your life to come to you. That's how you'll find peace. People think that they have to wage a kind of war in order to reach spiritual awareness. But it's all about paying attention at the right time."

Mike Zilinsky burst into the room, wearing gray sweat pants and a loose-fitting light blue T-shirt, acting as pumped as a boxer ready to enter the ring. Out of the corner of her eye, she saw the videographer hurriedly begin recording.

Just in time, because a stylish, solidly-built woman entered the room closely behind Zilinsky. Dr. Nyanga, whispered Tracy. The research director's clothes, a tailored charcoal and white-striped suit, offered a more professional appearance than that of her subject.

Two technicians huddled at a desk nearby over their laptops, tapping a mile a minute and muttering distractedly into headsets. They could be directing their conversations to one another, or to Siberia, for all Luz knew.

Amy had trusted Carla to the point that she would have gone through hell in a hut for the doctor. To satisfy Borlauch's bosses, Zilinsky would slather himself with the maximum amount of tech, but it did, as with Amy and Carla, come down to a simple matter of trust.

While Zilinsky settled into his chair and slipped on a headset, Nyanga spoke a few words about the need for witnesses to keep quiet during the entire procedure.

"If we have a match on the language, our people will let us know. All of you must practice maximum patience and try not to shout out guesses."

The lights, except for a single spotlight focused on Mike's chair, faded, as Nyanga injected him with the beta-anodynol.

Such an odd feeling came over Luz, as though she should drag him out of the chair, by force if necessary. She shouldn't have come.

THREE VERBAL AND NONVERBAL CUES IMPLANTED THUS FAR, EACH DESIGNED TO circumvent any roadblocks thrown up by the past life. If Mike heard Dr. Nyanga clap twice, or if she rubbed his nose, or said "A-hah," he would know to respond to her in English. Perhaps it would work.

I watched Mike's face get younger and younger each passing moment, the weight of years fleeing his body like gravity from an astronaut. His dazed toddler eyes shuttered, his hands and feet curled inward.

"Please come back," Rashida whispered.

I tuned back in.

"Michael, I want you to contact your past life. At no point are you to lose touch with me. You will remember to speak and understand English at all times. Do you understand?"

His chin rose briefly.

"At the count of three, go there. One, two, three."

A sudden gasp, his face became rigid with fear. Then the screams.

A galvanizing sound brought all of us out of our seats and Luz halfway down the aisle. I caught up to her and convinced her to sit back down.

When I looked at Mike again, Nyanga's repeated cues had sunk in. He looked back at her, calm now but exhausted, eyes reddened with tears.

"We'll have to skip that one and go to the next," he said shakily.

"What did you see?" Nyanga asked.

"Horrible things, nightmares, but they seemed real. Maybe she was schizophrenic."

"Describe those images."

"In my report. Later. Not now."

Nyanga looked worried. "Perhaps we should take a break."

"No, let's go through the drill again. I don't want to waste time."

Giving him an appraising look, she finally nodded. "I will stop whenever I deem it necessary."

The sinking inward, the cues, the moment. His eyes popped open and a stream of Spanish poured out of his lips, paused only by Nyanga's vigorous claps. Mike's familiar accent followed. Hallelujah.

"The memories I'm seeing now are of a cot in a ward. I see a lot of beds crammed in there with her. She's thirsty."

Nyanga asked an interpreter to join her on the podium.

We learned in short order that Concepcion Maria Duarte Apodaca, a middle-aged Dominican kitchen worker, loved cooking with her younger sister for the Don, loved taking care of the Don's grandchildren, and loved going to mass three times a week. She pined for Dolores Del Rio's autograph. She wasn't sure if the year was 1949 or 1950.

Chattering on about her life, Concepcion displayed little awareness of her environment. She referred once to Nyanga as "La Negrita Angel," but otherwise took her circumstances for granted. Father said, after all, that God, not man, designed heaven. All praise to Him and to baby Jesus and the Holy Virgin.

While the interpreter elicited more details from Concepcion, Luz whispered to us, "She's slow. Not severely, just slow."

"I don't understand," Tracy said, getting a hissed "sh-h-h" from the row behind us.

A little quieter, Tracy continued. "We're dealing spirit to spirit here, aren't we? So why is her spirit mentally challenged?"

Jiro shook his head. "Concepcion's soul is as healthy as yours, but the memories of her life are limited because she never grew up mentally. She seems like a spiritual person, but enlightenment is not the goal here at Borlauch. Nyanga sees each past life as a treasure trove. She wants to refine the procedure to where you harvest your past lives' language and abilities. You'd leave behind their personalities and habits, kind of like separating grains of rice from the hulls."

"You don't think that's possible, do you?" I felt aghast by the prospect.

"Maybe, but should it be done?" Jiro said. "I think there's a real possibility for spiritual growth if we transcended the cycle of death and forgetting."

"There's something to be said for not remembering everything." Luz turned her eyes toward Jiro. "Don't you think? Isao killed so many people. Amy treated herself like dirt most of her life. No honest comparison, I guess, but those were both destructive acts, committed over and over again."

"You'd rather not remember them?" I asked.

Nyanga and Mike pulled out of Concepcion's life, he received another injection, and they jumped back farther.

Luz stared at me, defiant. "I just don't like it, that's all. Look at them, picking and choosing which life they want to visit. They'd love for it to be Napoleon or someone like that."

The subject's eyes, clear and sane, surveyed the group. Snapping out a few choppy phrases, he waited for an answer. Claps from Nyanga brought forth Mike.

"I'm getting some strong memories of battle. Whoa, major action. Seems to be against a bunch of white guys in funny helmets."

Jiro cocked an eyebrow at Luz, who shrugged. "I've never heard that language before."

One of the technicians called out excitedly. "Dr. Nyanga, we've got a match. He's speaking Akan, a West African language, and what he's saying is that not even the white man's hell can contain a warrior of pure heart."

Mike nodded in agreement.

Rashida whacked me in the ribs, unable to control her excitement.

"Mama, that's the Ashanti. They kicked everyone's butt back in the day."

We all shushed her. Once they'd made the match, the voice-recognition software worked without a hitch, providing translations without having to wait for Mike's recaps. This allowed Nyanga to interrogate the persona named Osei for a few minutes as the beta-anodynol wore off. The memories became less and less vivid until Mike reappeared.

It had been quite a performance. And a performance it had been, intended for a select group of scientists and government officials. A more rigorous study would have trayed him in an advanced scanner to monitor clinical changes in his brain.

As though reading my mind, Jiro commented, "Over the next couple of days, they'll be debriefing him."

"What does that involve?" Luz asked.

"A lot of what Isao went through. Digging for facts that they can confirm independently. There's something else planned that will explore the question of neural plasticity."

"Yeah?" Luz said with more interest than she had thus far shown. "You've come up with a way to test it?"

"Not by myself. I've been working with two neuroscientists to develop methods. They'll have Mike listen to recordings of a past life's language while they measure how his brain reacts. It's called the evoked response potential, and it's impossible to fake. They'll identify the core phonemes or the key sounds and repeat the test during his regression to compare it to the base level."

Rashida's a smart kid but science has never been her forte. I could tell she felt confused by the discussion. I gave it a shot.

"The theory is that the drug changes the way the brain processes and acquires language. It makes the brain as malleable as that of a baby or a toddler. The test will give researchers one way to track the changes."

Jiro took over. "We'll also run an fMRI or functional MRI during a controlled regression in order to chart physiological changes in his brain. If all goes well, we'll attempt a merge, only this time under clinical conditions. I suspect that Mike will choose Osei."

Mike loved parachuting out of planes, rock-climbing, any activity with an element of danger, so why wouldn't he risk mental obliteration, especially in the cause of science. Furious at his stupidity, I told Rashida I would wait for her in the lobby and left.

I sank into a chair wedged between two enormous rubber plants and closed my eyes.

"Carla?" Mike's voice.

"Why aren't you back there taking a bow?"

Swathed in the afterglow of scaling the mountain, he beamed at me. I didn't return his rapturous smile.

"I need to go back in a little bit," he said. "I just wanted to talk to you, to explain why I'm going to do the merger."

"Don't bother explaining. Suicides never have a decent explanation for why they want to kill themselves."

He shook his head at me but didn't rise to the bait. "Once this drug is on the market, once word gets out that this is one of the potential uses, there'll be hundreds, maybe thousands of people like Amy. Most of them will be accidental, because some doctor somewhere wants to make a buck off it and doesn't want to follow the protocol. We have to find out if there's a safe way to guide the merging of personas, and we need to better understand the neurological effects."

"I didn't think anyone at Borlauch gave a damn about that."

He pulled a chair over and sat down in front of me.

"Carla, we've been studying the drug for many years. We didn't know about this particular aspect."

"It's not exactly a minor point, Mike. You don't know the long-term effects, let alone the short-term. What if you lose yourself?"

"Look, we could have merged Amy and Isao that first night had we known what was going on. Both the present and past personas have to be active participants in the process. Amy shut down; Isao was in a blind panic. He took over, and she hid.

"Even in the second session, we still didn't have a clue what to do. We focused on controlling or annihilating Isao when it would have been the equivalent of cutting off her legs without anesthesia. 'The operation was a success, but the patient died.' Once forced into an active state, we couldn't push Isao back into the bottle.

He gripped my hand. "Don't you see, Carla? All we have to do is open the door and guide the two together. They have no choice but to merge. Luz essentially did the job herself with no help from us. Now, we have to replicate it in a controlled setting."

"Which makes you John Glenn."

"More like the chimpanzee." His smile faded. "You know me."

"I should have brought Imani."

"I'll be back to see you guys."

"No, you won't. It will be an amalgam of you and someone who lived over a hundred years ago. It'll be a simulacrum—"

"It will be me," he interrupted my rant with a flash of anger. "You've had so much angst over Luz, obsessing over how much of Amy is still left, and how much is new. You've never seen the soul underneath it all. Call it a spirit, a conduit of energy, an intellectual essence. Call it whatever you want. You need to accept that a part of the Amy you loved and who loved you is still there.

"So what if I grab a few old lives and throw them in the blender. I'll still be in the mix. I promise you that I'll still love the girls and I'll still love you. Now, let's hug, because I've got to get back in there and finish schmoozing, okay?"

After we embraced and made plans for dinner later that evening, I turned and saw an overwhelmed Rashida nearby. She was nervously working the zipper in her suede jacket.

"What, baby," I said as she came toward us.

"I'm just starting to make sense of Japanese, and now I have to learn Ashanti."

"No, you don't, Ms. Brainiac," Mike tapped her on the forehead. "I'll still know English."

"Yeah, but I want you to really understand me."

"Don't worry, 'Shida. I've never had any problem understanding you, ever since you told me we were going to get married."

"I was only nine years old." She ducked behind me to avoid our amused scrutiny. "You have a memory like an elephant."

"Which kind?" I was struggling to spin down the tension, for Rashida's sake. "African or Asian?"

Mike and Rashida both answered, "African, of course."

Jiro insisted on Luz spending the night with him and his wife, a handsome Asian-American woman who was a fellow academic. She knew everything, most likely, but never let on.

The next day came a battery of tests: scans, blood work, even tests of her physical coordination. After they'd finished, Jiro drove her to O'Hare so she could make her flight.

"I'm glad you didn't make me try to juggle," she said while they waited at a light.

Jiro didn't respond. At the drop-off, he said quietly, "My wife's afraid I'll take the drug."

"Don't. That's my advice. Let Mike Zilinsky be the hero."

"My wife's afraid that my past life, that person may not be as nice as me. Her words, not mine," he said with a faint smile.

A car pulled up behind them and the driver honked, leaving no time for talk of soul-searching. Luz and Jiro got out and shook hands before parting.

Dr. Zilinsky was waiting for her at the terminal. She had hoped for Carla.

Sensing her disappointment, he said quickly, "Carla was afraid to call you. She felt she'd made such a botch of things the last time you two were around each other."

"Around each other." Such lovely manners. "No harm, no foul."

"I know you're in a hurry, but the doctors had you so tied up today, I couldn't get anywhere near you. I want to know if you think I'm crazy."

He had the air of a man wanting a reason to back out.

"I think if beta-anodynol's going out on the market, then what you're doing is necessary. And brave. I could never volunteer to do something like that."

"But you did. Not volunteer, but you did go through it."

She clasped him on the shoulder. "I hope you like Osei. You better have a strong stomach. War is nothing like the movies. It's boring, it's frustrating, it's bloody, and your friends have a bad habit of dying in your lap. That's not even the worst of what's ahead. If you do this, Osei will see parts of you no one has ever seen."

"He'll know me like a lover."

"It's nothing that shallow. Lovers just know the bathroom details, how petty you are, your idiosyncrasies. Osei will know things you've never faced up to in your life, things you don't even know are still buried in your mind."

The flight attendants began ushering passengers through the gate.

"Have you accepted them?" He kept pace with her as she approached the gate.

"Accepted what?"

"The worst parts of Isao and Amy."

"They've made me who I am today."

He brought her to a standstill.

"They. You always say 'they.' It's never 'we,' or 'when I was serving in the Army,' or 'when I taught school.' Always 'they.' 'They' made the mistakes, not you. You never killed anyone. You didn't try to starve yourself to death. You're thinking you're the pure one. You're the virgin birth."

Passengers dawdled as they passed by, trying to listen in. The son of a bitch.

She shoved him back a few feet, which failed to slow his tempo.

"I've done awful things in my life, too," Zilinsky said. "I've thought about what it's going to be like, to spend the rest of my life so profoundly changed. One thing I won't do is pretend I'm not the jerk who screwed around on his wife so much she left him. Let me tell you, that's the least of my sins."

A handsome, oh-so-earnest man. He would be an excellent spokesman for Borlauch. That is, if Osei didn't so alter his priorities that he became an artist instead. A flight attendant tapped him on the shoulder. Time to get out of the way of air commerce.

"You may be right, Zilinsky, but let me know when you get on the other side, and we'll talk again."

Her mood a strange mixture of compassion and irritation, she stroked his face and said softly, "You have no idea what you're getting into."

He looked back at her, confounded, as she turned on her heels and blew out of town.

TWENTY TWO

THE FIRST ARTIFACT TO GO WAS HER LEGAL NAME. WITH THE HELP OF GORDON'S lawyer and a sympathetic judge, Luz made the change official, going from Amy Duran to Luz Bernard, that being her maternal grandmother's maiden name. The judge ordered the court documents to be sealed. She had already placed her house on the market.

Nina hated the next step, complaining, even as she helped box up books, that Luz didn't know anyone in Seattle. "Besides, your son's not even a citizen. They might go back to Japan tomorrow and then what'll you do? Move to Tokyo?"

"This isn't about Masao. All I'm doing is renting an apartment while I look for work."

"Liar. But Seattle's a pretty place. You'll love it."

The view at Regala was less inviting, as her boss hyperblinked himself into a tizzy over her resignation. She could have continued her work from anywhere, but best to leave a cold trail for potential snoops.

Most of her belongings now in storage, her mail switched to Nina's address, she had nothing left to do except get on the plane and reinvent herself. And say goodbye to Carla.

———

FOR WEEKS AFTER THE MERGING OF PERSONAS, MIKE SAID VERY LITTLE TO ME about the experience, or about anything else, for that matter. Jiro chalked it up to system shock, the result of a crash merge rather than Luz's gradual process.

In time, Mike's calls and e-mails regained a portion of their former liveliness, albeit with some odd sentence constructs and tangents.

Osei worked as a goldsmith before having to defend Kumasi, the capital of the Ashantis. He possessed a visceral hatred of Englishmen, a prejudice not altogether diminished by the merge. How fortunate that Mike's ancestors hailed from Eastern European ghettos. He planned to take a trip soon to Austin. Osei's history as a family man made the new construct even more interested in how the girls were doing.

I was shooting hoops in the driveway one afternoon with Imani and two of her friends. Having backed one boy into the garage door, my baby daughter was busy scraping him off the driveway—he didn't seem to mind—when Rashida ran outside to tell me the news.

Borlauch's first mistake had been thinking they could buy Faye Marin's temporary silence. CNN's Web site blazed with news of a breathtaking discovery in the field of past-life research.

Borlauch's second mistake? Believing Marin would be the only potential threat. A Borlauch researcher, devoutly Catholic, went on the record to denounce the procedure. This gave Marin the catbird seat of "reluctantly" coming forth with details that would land her on the homepage of *Time* and many other media Web sites.

That night, I didn't hear my name on TV, but I knew my luck wouldn't last.

My phone rang while I was trying to explain the past few months to a justifiably upset Imani.

I stepped out of the room to take the call. Luz calmly announced her plans to leave for Seattle the next morning.

"Have you been paying attention to the news today?" I asked her.

"No, I've been busy. Why?"

She took the news well enough. She offered her concern that I would get outed in the process.

"Not if Marin has anything to do with it. She'd hate to give me any credit."

"All the same, I'm glad I'm leaving. I'd like for us to meet. I'm over at Nina's."

A visit, chaperoned by her friend. It sounded safe.

We sat outside on the back porch and watched Nina try to teach her Akita puppy to roll over on command. Nina gauged my mood in an instant and moved over to the puppy training in order to leave us alone.

Autumn in Austin takes a long time to get serious. It pretends to be summer until it decides to shed some leaves and immediately sprint for winter. The air felt like last spring, before everything happened.

"What will you do in Seattle?" I asked Luz.

"Pick up some work translating. I should do okay since there are lots of

Pacific Rim businesses in the area."

There didn't seem to be an appropriate moment for saying what I needed to say, so I went ahead and blurted out an apology for my behavior. This provoked a tolerant smile from her.

"Carla, I'm not the only one who's been a head case lately. We've all been through a lot. I want to know one thing. Did you love Amy?"

"I couldn't allow myself to consider that possibility."

"Did you love me? Before?" Luz persisted, looking more amused than impatient.

"Yes."

"That's why you picked Amy, why you picked me, for the study. You believed Mike about the drug, and you thought it would help. You did it out of love. It wasn't your fault about what happened the next night."

Leaning over, she gave me a kiss that started slow and took its time to finish.

"Now I'm leaving, just when the media's about to descend. Not very thoughtful, am I?" she said in a voice all warm notes and mellow highlights.

A weaker person would have asked her to stay. "Don't worry about me. Marin is not about to give my name any play."

She cocked her head at me. "From here on out, Marin has no control over the situation. Trust me on this. Get an unlisted number and move if you have to. Be ready, because pretty soon you're not going to have a private life."

"I hope you will. Have a private life." With or without me, I added silently.

"Don't worry." A flashed, furtive smile. "I used to break necks for a living, remember?"

TWENTY THREE

It is living and ceasing to live that are imaginary solutions. Existence is elsewhere.
—André Breton

BY THE TIME TV SATELLITE TRUCKS BEGAN CLUSTERING OUTSIDE MY OFFICE, I HAD changed my phone numbers and e-mail, accepted a friend's offer for the girls to stay with them for a while, and tried again to explain to Imani how my wanting to prove Marin wrong caused all this to happen.

Imani was angry that she hadn't been told, angrier still that Uncle Mike had gone through the same procedure. She gave Rashida and me the silent treatment for days.

The same anger seeped through Masao Watanabe's sole press conference, which he conducted standing next to his diplomat son in front of the Japanese consulate.

He blasted Borlauch for: a) disturbing his father's rest, and b) not telling him his father had returned. A handsome, gray-haired man, Masao spoke English well enough to convey the absurdity of the situation.

"Excuse me," he said at one point. "My father's dead and yet now they say he's alive. Alive, in an American who's much younger than I. You ask, do I want to see my father? My memories don't include him looking like a woman."

I lost several clients, but gained others. I collected hate mail and hostile looks, publishing offers, and talk-show invitations. Many politicians, news columnists, and religious leaders joined in condemning both the procedure and me, although some pitched the notion that I had merely been an unwitting tool of Borlauch.

The new head of the NAACP took umbrage at the tone of some of the remarks and released a statement calling me an African-American researcher who made a breakthrough that "all people, regardless of their ethnicity, should acknowledge is an extraordinary achievement."

All during the first week.

Then on a crisp Monday morning, Dr. Nyanga appeared before a phalanx of news cameras and introduced Mike as the "co-discoverer of the procedure, as well as a brave pioneer in the continuing effort to better understand the precious gift of life God has given us."

More carefully worded piety followed. Mike seemed at ease with himself, inclined to joke back and forth with the reporters. His mannerisms, even his accent, had changed almost beyond recognition.

Asked by one reporter if he had any plans for after the furor had passed, he leaned forward on the table and said into the camera, "I intend to go visit a friend, shoot darts, and have a good time. Some things will never change."

AFTER CHECKING INTO A CHEAP MOTEL, THE MORE ANONYMOUS THE BETTER, LUZ drove over to the nearest barbershop and paid for a major trim.

Afterward, feeling almost weightless, she inserted a pair of light gray contact lenses purchased back in Austin. She used the rearview mirror to check her handiwork. It definitely changed her appearance, but would the change be enough?

It helped that Luz had added a little bit of dance muscle, which, combined with the hairstyle, made her look more like an ex-jock than ex-teacher. She hoped.

The next day, while eating her morning bagel at a downtown coffee shop, she saw herself on the morning newscast. It was only a question of when, not whether, she would be drawn into the fray.

"The first person to experience a documented regression, and the first person to experience a mind meld," the announcer said.

Mind meld? Sounded Vulcan. Trying not to cringe, Luz peeked at the other customers as they watched a thin woman burst out of her chair, shrieking in Japanese that he would not be taken prisoner again. Clips of the Brackenridge session followed and then a photograph taken for her personnel tag at Bookish filled the screen. The long hair had served to lengthen her face and accentuate the gauntness.

The segment over, she asked the man next to her for the name of a good restaurant. Luz looked him straight in the eye. Not a trace of recognition.

That afternoon, she drove over to the Japanese consulate and left her resume with the receptionist, who was a young woman wearing too much makeup. She had coached both Ben and Nina in what to say if contacted. Yes, Luz Bernard is an excellent translator-for-hire, adept in four languages. Further references available upon request. (Please don't call.)

While at the consulate, she studied brochures on a side table. Maybe Isao's grandson, Akira, might happen to pass through. Masao might even drop by for a visit. Maybe her plan was a total pipe dream.

The receptionist's eyes were boring a hole through Luz. A strategic retreat appeared to be in order. She collected a couple of travel brochures and started to leave, only to see a well-muscled Japanese man in a navy business suit come from a hallway behind the desk. He struck up a conversation with the receptionist about an upcoming party.

"Oh," the receptionist said in English. "Ms. Bernard?"

Continuing in Japanese, she said in a skeptical voice, "She *says* she knows four languages. She's worked as a guide."

The man's accent was a dead giveaway to his origins. Luz asked him in deliberately speeded up Japanese, "Have you been home to Kyoto lately, honorable sir? I've read that the baseball team is doing very well."

His eyes widened with surprise. "If we didn't have to play the Giants, we'd be doing fine. I'm sure that's your team." He picked her resume up off the desk and gave a casual glance. "My name's Kazue Inamoto. Do you really speak four languages?"

"English, Mandarin, Spanish, and, of course, Japanese."

"What brings you to Seattle?"

"Opportunity."

She needed to come up with a better explanation. He had the receptionist pencil her in for an interview with the assistant to the chief attaché the next morning.

"If you don't mind me asking, what's the assistant's name?"

A low chuckle. "Kazue Inamoto."

Back at the motel, she heard a knock on the door just as she was about to step into the shower. She threw on shorts and a T-shirt before looking through the peephole. Tracy Hara, Miss Friendly from the Zilinsky session. So much for hiding.

Over veggie wraps at a nearby stand, Tracy said that her agency had known all along she would bail and probably for Seattle. "It was easy enough. You still have the same car, the same license plates. Why send anyone on low pursuit? Where else would you come but here?"

"Why are you following me, and who do you work for?"

"It's nothing personal, Luz. Live your life. We're not interfering one bit. We're not going to ask you to do anything, none of that cloak and dagger stuff. Like the talking heads say, you're the first. It's my job to make sure you don't get mugged and end up at the bottom of the bay."

"Thanks a lot."

"Show some appreciation, girl." Tracy acted mock-hurt for a moment, but returned to her customary breeziness.

"Believe me, once there's more of you lifers in circulation, there won't be any need for this. Those idiots at Borlauch wanted to keep you in that psych ward long term. They were lining up a judge to sign the order. It freaked them out that you might disappear on them. I'm glad Dr. Zilinsky called us. We agreed to keep a close watch on you in exchange for certain considerations on research. I don't know if you realize just how big a deal this is."

"I changed my name and left town. That should be an indication."

"Not bad for an amateur. Just a little advice. Don't approach your son too soon. From what I hear, he would've packed up and left for Tokyo if not for your grandson talking him out of it."

According to the consulate's Web site, her grandson, Akira, was married with two children. Masao had another son living back in Japan. I'm a great-grandfather, she thought. For a woman who's never been pregnant, that's the definition of "hell-no" improbable.

"I don't know if I'll ever get up the nerve to tell Masao," Luz said.

It could have been worse, she thought. Instead of a chirpy surfer girl, her bodyguard could have been the Bruce Willis type. She wondered if Tracy was packing a gun in her bag.

"You'll tell him someday." Tracy's expression turned serious. "Human nature doesn't change much. Maybe from life to life, but Isao had a lot of guts to change careers when he did, and Amy basically tossed everything out the window after she went into therapy."

"You know a lot about me."

"It's my job. Do you want the other wrap?"

"Guess."

TWENTY FOUR

I BEGAN RECEIVING CHATTY E-MAILS FROM LUZ WEEKS AFTER SHE MOVED. HER part-time job at the consulate blossomed into a full-blown position. Her cost-efficient boss loved the idea of sending her with various Japanese dignitaries up and down the coast, as well as into Mexico.

She saw her grandson, Akira Watanabe, surprisingly often in the course of her job, but she was careful to maintain a professional attitude with him. For a career diplomat, Akira revealed an off-beat sense of humor, and liked to show off photos of his children's school events.

A retiree who liked to check in on consulate doings, Masao occasionally crossed paths with Luz. After each occasion, her e-mails were breathless with detail. Her son was handsome, dignified, and warm.

Imani decided to forgive me in time for Mike's visit over the holidays. It was an intimate affair, capped off by his giving each of us small silver engraved cups.

"Gold's too expensive to work with," he explained. "Back in the old days, you could do a whole chair in gold, including the footstool."

Spoken with authority by a man who remembered when Queen Victoria ruled the British Empire, the brutal fist within her genteel glove.

He had started attending synagogue services on a regular basis.

"It's funny, I guess, but it means more to me now than it used to. You wouldn't think that, but it's true," he said. "It's not even Osei's religion, but he was such a spiritual man. I never made a move without checking first with the gods."

"How does he feel about being Jewish?" Rashida asked.

"How do I feel?" Mike corrected her. "Great."

"Isn't it confusing?" Imani asked.

"Not really. Maybe everyone during the service is praying with all their lives, all in that moment. I like to think that."

"It sounds crowded." Imani looked dubious.

He smiled at her encouragingly. "I'm not a rabbi; I'm just Joe Schmo."

"Is that another past life?" Rashida teased.

"I'm living it right now."

Mike tried to contact Toni Akugawa during his stay with us, without success. During the media onslaught, she condemned Borlauch, myself, and Mike in that order. Her high moral stance did not prevent her, however, from being the second to sign a book deal, right behind Faye Marin.

How relaxed Mike had been in the tavern, tossing darts with deadly accuracy, yet contriving to miss when my aim went wide more than twice in a row. The old Mike would never have done that. Given to long stretches of introspection, Mike still seemed to be working on what it meant to have what Borlauch now called an "enhanced personality."

At one point during the game of darts, I happened to look over at him and finally noticed another of the changes. Always, he'd been youthfully handsome, if a bit too self-possessed, but now, a worn maturity infused his face. I hoped Osei's gravitas wouldn't end up fossilizing my friend. Although I knew now that Mike was still with me, I didn't want my friend to lose his zest for the life he was currently experiencing.

Rashida enrolled in Beginning Japanese II when classes started back up again in January. Possibly due to Rashida's influence, Randall's grades improved and his partying diminished, both of which had to be welcome events to Gordon.

When my daily crush of calls and visits began to ease, the office manager decided not to quit after all. But a couple of my patients proved to be not so forgiving, upset by my refusal to provide them with a beta-anodynol quickie.

The Borlauch researcher primarily responsible for developing beta-anodynol was named *Time* magazine's Man of the Year. His modesty, Borlauch's secretiveness, and my lack of curiosity were to blame, but still, I should have wondered why Dr. Jiro Endo took such a personal involvement in the events of last summer. Other than an interview on Rachel Maddow's show, he avoided the spotlight. Mike's growing prominence in media coverage made that task much easier for me.

In the spring, I received a letter from the Japanese consulate in Seattle in which Masao Watanabe, Isao's son, invited me up for a visit. Since much of the Japanese media spotlight fell on him and his family, he had been unable to move freely in the early months. However, the camera crews returned to Tokyo upon news that a Borlauch-owned Japanese subsidiary had launched a large-scale study of induced past-life regressions.

According to Masao, many Japanese, influenced by the Buddhist tradition, wanted to examine their past lives for tell-tale signs of karma at work in order to neutralize its ill effects in their present lives. Despite my own theories on the subject, blame and causation remained a popular explanation for next-life destinations.

Masao expected the medical establishment in Japan to approve beta-anodynol for general use under a physician's supervision.

I read about riots in India among the Untouchables, who protested their government's ban on the drug. Most of the Islamic world banned the drug outright, except for Malaysia and Indonesia.

At home, the reaction ran the gamut, with the usual hysteria in the usual quarters. The FDA proceeded with the planned indications for substance abuse treatment and granted approval in early January for use of beta-anodynol in treatment for various addictive and obsessive-compulsive behaviors. It advised Borlauch to proceed with caution on other avenues of research.

Congress tabled a proposed bill banning past-life studies after strong protests by the committee's chairman, who represented the Illinois district that Borlauch called home.

A CNN poll found the public sharply divided on induced regressions, with fifty-four percent in favor and forty-four percent opposed.

Only two percent had no opinion at all.

IT WAS A GLITTERING, CHANDELIER-LIT SETTING FOR THE CONSULATE PARTY. Couples, dressed in formal evening attire, glided across a polished dance floor to the accompaniment of a four-piece jazz combo.

Luz loved the high arched ceilings, which was a nice aspect to holding an event in what had been an Episcopal church. She turned her gaze toward the waiters, who flowed with trained effortlessness through the crowd.

She wished that she could achieve the same elegance in her simple-black-dress-single-strand-of-pearls ensemble. She'd rather be in a tank and cutoffs.

Everywhere, it seemed, a corporate leader from Japan wanted to communicate with the Beijing trade representative, or a Mexican industrialist craved a tête-à-tête with the chief attaché. No one trusted their English for the occasion, so Luz received frequent requests to help.

Her pro wrestler-sized comrade, Kazue Inamoto, winked at her jovially. "How are you enjoying the party?"

He allowed her to steal his drink.

"I've turned down two offers of marriage and an outright pass, thank you very much."

"Good for you. Maybe you should hold out for the guest of honor."

"The Chinese trade rep? I don't think so." Eighty years old, from the looks of it, and ugly as a toad.

"You should listen to gossip more often, Luz. The man who invented the reincarnation super drug is expected to come."

Jiro Endo? "Why? I mean, why here?"

"They're keeping it hush-hush, but I heard that Dr. Endo wants to meet with Akira and his father, so the chief attaché's going to use the occasion to give him a plaque."

"Why do they care?"

Did Jiro plan to tell Masao the truth about her? What on earth was going on?

"A little detail like him being a Canadian citizen who's lived in the States for years, that's not going to stop our beloved leaders from taking all the credit they can for Tsuru."

That was the just-announced Japanese brand name for beta-anodynol. Tsuru was the word for crane, a bird that signified long life.

"Since we have Old Man China as our number two honored guest, is there a better moment?" Kazue said as he stole his drink back from Luz.

"I guess not."

One-upsmanship appeared to be a universal trait. Out of the corner of her eye, she saw Akira crooking his finger in her direction.

She hurried over, struck by how handsome her grandson looked tonight in his black tuxedo and the latest fashion accessory, a koi-print cummerbund. He was so unaffected with others. As for his wife, standing beside him, what a good, faithful woman. Intelligent, too. Not a mere trophy bauble.

Akira greeted her with a kindly smile.

"Dr. Endo is over by the door with Dr. Turner, so please go over and introduce yourself. See to it that no one monopolizes his time. I'll let you know when we're ready to make the presentation."

She mumbled something she hoped sounded like agreement and headed for Jiro and yes, Carla. She felt a state of shock setting in. Carla said she might be up to visit soon, but a little warning would have been nice. Why wouldn't Jiro want to meet Masao, and why wouldn't her little experiment blow up in her face?

Too cute by half.

She had fallen into a comfortable routine in Seattle. She enjoyed sketching geese in the park on sunny days and listening to cafe singers on rainy days. She went dancing with Kazue, a big man surprisingly light on his feet who found it convenient to date a woman who didn't press for intimacy—the chief attaché not being a noted proponent of gay equality.

It had been such a nice little life she constructed, crumbling brick by brick as she walked over to Jiro and Carla.

JIRO WHISPERED, "SHE MOVES SO WELL."

Lord, yes. Yet, without the full-throttle brashness of the woman who danced with all comers at that club. Her hair trimmed and given subtle highlights, she advanced upon us with the solemn air of a trooper on dawn patrol.

Perhaps I should have warned her, but Jiro insisted on making it a surprise. Although I always liked the natural color of her eyes, translucent gray gave her a striking look, one that drew appreciative stares as she walked by.

"Hiding in plain sight," I remarked to Jiro.

"Hmm?"

"A woman you can't take your eyes off couldn't possibly be the woman everyone is looking for."

"Not everyone is looking for her," he said.

"I meant that metaphorically."

Luz dipped her head in an abbreviated bow and offered a formal welcome to Seattle. That much I understood, but the rest slipped into movie Japanese, pregnant with meaning but well beyond my grasp. A burly Japanese man glided over from the buffet table, told her something, and then sped off.

"Dr. Endo, Dr. Turner, if you would come with me. The chief attaché's ready for you now."

I couldn't help but smile at her stiff formality, which prompted a fiercely whispered, "Carla, you better behave yourself."

"Or you'll send your grandson after me?"

A look of pride came over her face. "You'll love him. My e-mails don't do him justice. He really should be the one running the consulate. He's a wonderful man, he loves his wife and kids, and he's crazy about baseball."

"He doesn't suspect a thing?"

"Why should he? Now, shut it."

After I posed for photographs with Luz studiously out of the shot, I ate sausage balls that, despite the Pacific Rim element, seemed to be the tidbit of choice. I danced with three stolid men in succession and chatted about the future of beta-anodynol with various tuxedos before managing to work my way back around to Jiro and Luz. Jiro huddled with Akira, Luz's grandson, while Luz sat a few yards away with a bemused expression on her face.

"How's your night working out?" I asked as I pulled over a chair and sat down beside her.

"Thus far, I've managed to stay out of the photo ops, which isn't too hard, since I'm obviously not anyone important."

"You could change that."

"I don't want to. Not yet, anyway." Casting her eyes over to the near corner, she smiled ruefully. "I wondered how she'd get in."

"Who?" Glancing over in that direction, I saw a bubbly woman holding forth to a pair of admirers.

"My bodyguard. You saw her at Mike's session. I guess she swung an invitation."

"She works for the feds?" The agent was another believer in the make-yourself-obvious school of camouflage.

Luz ignored the question. "What's Jiro up to?"

"Talking to your grandson."

"I think Akira wants to talk Jiro into moving to Tokyo. Mucho yen. Jiro had to have set this up."

"Why?"

"To make the formal introduction, what do you think? He'll probably sneak us off to a broom closet and hit Akira with the news, then use him to work on my son."

"What's wrong with that?"

"It's too soon. I need more time. Masao barely knows me."

Something in her eyes, the wary good humor, made me take a chance. "I was wondering if maybe we could start over, you and I."

Her eyes widened. "Carla, I don't know that we ever really got started in the first place, and now, there's this issue of you being a public figure, and me..."

"Not wanting to be," I finished. "I understand. I don't want to complicate your life anymore than I already have. It's just that—"

"There are unresolved issues, yeah."

"I love you." I said that a little louder than I intended, but no one turned their heads. The music provided a protective envelope.

"What?"

"I love you. Now."

"Carla, you need to give me a little more time." She softened her words with a brilliant smile. "Not too much longer."

The tension in her face abruptly went up a few notches. I turned and saw Akira approaching, accompanied by a man who looked like he could be—yes, Masao.

IN THE NOW

———————————

SHE SLIPPED BACK INTO HER HEELS AND STOOD UP AS THE TWO MEN APPROACHED.

"Ah, Luz, have you worn out your feet tonight?" Masao inquired.

"No, sir."

"Good. I saw you dancing with Kazue. It's now my turn."

Masao guided her onto the dance floor before she could develop an alibi. Thank God, a mid-tempo Latin number, nothing too complicated, and wasn't it a good thing Masao had inherited Isao's sense of rhythm. What if he made a pass? Of course, he wouldn't. She reminded herself of the age difference.

A wave of panic crested, then subsided. Something inside her righted itself. This is my son, she thought, mentally splashing water on herself. I'm not going to embarrass him.

"Luz?" He pulled her closer.

"Yes?"

"I know who you are."

Adrenaline flushed from her pores. She wondered if she looked as stunned as she felt.

He gazed at her affectionately. "Come now. Let's try to stay with the beat."

"How did you... why didn't you tell me?"

"Akira worried that you were a fake or simply misguided. Was Borlauch connected with your showing up here? We weren't sure at first. I read the research and talked to Jiro Endo. After speaking with him, I had Kazue drive me around recently so I could follow you on your day off."

He smiled. "You probably don't recall the occasion, but you were at a market picking out fruit. There was music playing from a radio. It only lasted a few seconds but you danced. There was a child, I think belonging to the fruit seller. You took her hand, and you danced for a moment. That's when I knew."

Masao's eyes were gleaming with tears threatening to overflow. "You danced with me the same way. Always smiling, always laughing. Mother never said a good word about you until the year before she died. She confessed how she slept with other men and that it was her fault you got so drunk that night. She told me she killed you."

His arms were shaking from emotion. Luz had to get them off the dance floor. She took him over to a quiet corner by the sorely neglected sushi bar.

"Masao." She started, faltered, and regrouped. "I died because of too much scotch and a truck driver who couldn't brake fast enough. I loved your mother so much I couldn't see that she was a girl who married too young to a man she didn't love. All because she wanted to upset your grandfather. You were the best part, the only good part of our marriage. You were my beautiful boy, my Masao. I loved coming home to you, but you were so young, I don't see how you'd remember anything about me."

"But I do. I wasn't a baby. I never believed what she said about you. Uncle told me you were a good man. A very good man."

At the periphery of her vision, she noticed Carla and Akira on opposite sides of them, providing cover.

Masao continued. "That's why I suggested to Akira we have this ceremony. He contacted Jiro Endo before getting the chief attaché on board. I wanted to meet the people who brought my father back to me. I know that you were once a shy lady who worked in a bookstore and that you have a brother and nephew you love very much. We're your family here, but I want you to be able to see the others and not be afraid."

"You don't have to hide." Carla's voice came from behind Luz's shoulder.

"That's right, Grandfather," Akira said eagerly. "I can set up an interview with NHK and CNN."

"No." Luz fought to control her rising panic.

"You won't be alone," Akira told her. "We'll be there to help. We'll invite two or three reporters for an exclusive. We'll stage it at the consulate, make it an undercover exclusive, and fly you out of town afterward."

Luz hedged. "I don't know."

"I've already cleared it with the agent assigned to you," Akira said.

Tracy Hara was sipping on a glass of wine just a few feet away. She was chatting with Kazue, but both of them seemed on high alert. Luz finally realized that Kazue must serve as the consulate's undercover security counterpart to Tracy, which accounted for why he had been so friendly all along. She felt particularly clueless at that moment. Everyone had been in on the secret.

"Where would I go?"

"My wife's family has a vacation home in Montana." Jiro's hand rested softly on her shoulder. "It's beautiful up there this time of year."

It moved her, seeing them work so hard to fix an impossible situation, knowing that whatever they did, she would lose the last shred of a pretense at being a private citizen. This way, at least, she would have the illusion of control for a while.

Dear, loyal Carla spoke up. "And think, Luz, you'll finally get your life back."

"Which one?"

EPILOGUE

Time is the substance from which I am made. Time is a river that carries me along, but I am the river; it is a tiger that devours me, but I am the tiger; it is a fire that consumes me, but I am the fire.

—Jorge Luis Borges

LUZ REMEMBERED LITTLE OF THE INTERVIEW, EXCEPT THAT THE REPORTERS fumbled over their words at first, seemingly in awe of her.

The only moments clear in her memory were those spent that afternoon with Masao and his—their—family in which they talked about relatives, school, her experiences during the war, and acting on TV during the early '60s. Whenever she slowed down, afraid that she was boring them, her great-grandchildren urged her on.

"What next, what next?" they'd eagerly asked.

Both children, teenagers, really, shared their e-mail addresses and phone numbers. They found it hard to believe that Luz knew how to text and Tweet until she demonstrated her thumbing skills. Forget how Isao survived World War II. Great-grandfather knew about modern communications. That had impressed them.

Now, she was waiting out the media storm in a cabin that felt more like a luxury suite except for an Ansel Adams-sized view of the Rockies.

She wondered what would happen next. Tracy and another agent took turns staying with her. They always found ways of disappearing when the need for solitude came upon her. Carla, Gordon, Randall, and Nina—everyone who loved her wanted to be there, but it was safer for them to stick to phone calls and e-mail.

Jiro's advice had been to let life come to her. But from the moment Isao ran on Amy's feet through a humid Austin night, she had been bouncing off all obstacles and trying whatever tangent that worked.

She had gotten back into the habit of praying. The mood would strike while she was on a walk or getting ready for bed.

"Today I saw a couple of hawks attack a smaller bird. I guess they had their reasons. I'm almost through with that book by Shiga. Another classic I'd never gotten around to. And the sunset, thanks for the sunset today. It was lovely."

One morning she was skipping rocks across the surface of a pond near the cabin when she realized that she didn't have to know whether Amy's God, the voice in the burning bush, existed.

She remembered the second session where Amy saw a golden light on the horizon and had placed her hand in a ribbon of fire. Amy had felt no pain, only an impression of something that sounded like exhilaration and looked like joy.

When Luz died, that ribbon of fire would take her in.

In a recent e-mail, Mike/Osei described his grand experiment. He wanted to take beta-anodynol whenever he knew he was dying and see if it were possible to link up safely to his next life. He wanted to leap across the chasm and be born truly self-aware.

He also planned to merge with another one of his earlier lives, an Indian farmer named Nayal. Not that he needed her opinion, but she pointed out that he might not have as much cargo space in his head as he believed.

There would be others wanting to collect the dreams of all their previous lives, doing it simply because now they could, not because they felt compelled to understand those dreams.

Did she dream this life? Was all this tumult and struggle nothing more than a brief interlude in a millennium-long slumber? To wake up an eternity from now and know that all she considered important had long since turned to dust?

Rising to her feet, she saw Tracy farther down on the bank, trying to unsnarl a fishing line.

"Luz, are you going to help me fish?"

"In a bit. I'm going for a run. Want to come?"

"Sure. Where we headed?" Tracy laid down her rod and shrugged off her jacket.

Luz pointed at a stand of trees some distance down the road.

"Let's start there and build up. After that, who knows, maybe to Butte."

"Or the moon."

Luz thought it over.

"Perhaps."

ABOUT THE AUTHOR

In addition to Sinclair's SF work for Lethe and general fiction with Regal Crest, the Texas Panhandle native is also a political writer for People's World magazine, and an audio reviewer for Library Journal. As a singer-songwriter, she's written for herself (*Alive in Soulville*) as well as others. She's also a computer artist. She lives in Temple, Texas, and is associated with the website asebomedia.net.

For more information, email kelly57anat@yahoo.com